MOSSBELLY MACFEARSOME

AND THE DWARVES OF DOOM

First published in Great Britain in 2019 by
Andersen Press Limited
20 Vauxhall Bridge Road
London SW1V 2SA
www.andersenpress.co.uk

2 4 6 8 10 9 7 5 3

British Library Cataloguing in Publication Data available.

ISBN 978 1 78344 791 6

This book is printed on FSC accredited paper
from responsible sources

Printed and bound in Great Britain by Clays Ltd,
Elcograf S.p.A.

MOSSBELLY MACFEARSOME

AND THE DWARVES OF DOOM

ALEX GARDINER

ANDERSEN PRESS

Look out for:

Mossbelly MacFearsome and the Goblin Army

For Molly

Prologue

Queen Gwri looked at the warrior in front of her. 'Are you ready?' she asked.

Mossbelly MacFearsome nodded. 'I am ready.'

'You have the covert cloak?'

'In here.' The warrior patted the black satchel hanging over his right hip.

'Is it working?'

'Yes-ish. As well as can be expected. It's a long-ago thing.'

'You should not go by yourself, without companions,' said the Queen.

Mossbelly MacFearsome shook his head. 'I must go alone. You know the reason. No one can know our plan.' He puffed out his chest. 'And I am equal to a hundred companions.'

'But the danger!'

'It must be attempted. I will succeed.'

'You have the hammer?' Queen Gwri asked.

The warrior pointed at the satchel, slapped his chest, and then tapped a finger, twice, on the side of his nose.

'You cannot do the deed yourself,' said the Queen. 'You must find a suitable human to be your Destroyer.'

'I know, I know,' said Mossbelly MacFearsome, nodding.

'And you know where the Witchwatcher dwells?'

'I have the name of her castle.'

'Weapons?'

'Do not worry for me.'

'But I do. He will come for you, to kill you. And I am powerless to help, unless you can destroy—'

'It is the plan, to risk my death at his hands.' The warrior's voice grew deeper. He leaned forward and gently touched the large wart on the end of the Queen's nose. 'Rule well, my beloved. Farewell.'

A tear trickled down the Queen's face. 'Farewell,' she whispered, turning to leave.

Mossbelly MacFearsome, Captain of the Royal Guard, took a deep breath and watched as the love of his life walked away on her backward-facing feet.

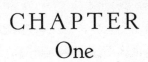

CHAPTER
One

Roger Paxton's stomach was churning. He was scared. Hugh Ball was waiting for him at the park, looking for revenge.

It had all started when Roger had intervened as Hugh was twisting another boy's arm. In front of the entire playground, Roger had shouted at Hugh and called him an *unmitigated bully*. He wasn't really sure what *unmitigated* meant, but he had heard someone else saying it. And it had worked. Hugh had stopped his attack on the boy and turned his attention to Roger. Fortunately, before Hugh could inflict any damage, a teacher had intervened and saved Roger. But a message, to meet Hugh at the park at four o'clock, *or else*, had been delivered during the afternoon break.

Roger looked at his watch. It was five past four on Friday. He could turn the next corner and meet Hugh, or he could turn round and go home. Meeting Hugh would end in considerable pain. But going home would only prolong what he would eventually have to face, on Monday morning, to save Hugh's reputation as the undisputed school bully.

Roger sighed and began walking towards the park. He had only taken a couple of steps when he bumped into something hard and unyielding. He staggered back and stood looking at . . . what? Roger blinked.

There was nothing there.

He held out both hands and felt the empty air. There was a loud grunt followed by the sound of heavy footsteps. Roger began to walk away quickly.

Behind him someone sniff-snorted. Roger spun round.

From out of nowhere, a dwarf appeared. A dwarf, who looked as though he had just stepped out of a fantasy film.

'Where did you come from?' gasped Roger.

The dwarf looked puzzled. 'Can you see me?' he asked, raising his arms and looking down at himself as he turned his body from side to side.

Roger nodded vigorously. He was looking at a dwarf wearing a flimsy, see-through cloak and hood. Under the cloak the dwarf was dressed in a brown leather tunic with matching trousers tucked into scuffed boots. The dwarf was almost as broad as he was tall. He had a wrinkly,

4

leathery face, covered in faint blue marks, and a long grey beard. There was a sword, dagger and a knobbly cudgel on one side of his waist, and a bulky black satchel hanging on the other side. A two-headed axe was strapped to his lower chest and Roger caught a glimpse of a small black hammer nestling just under his beard as the dwarf moved his body.

'Yes,' said Roger, still nodding.

'Are you sure?' asked the dwarf in a deep, rumbling voice. His accent was of someone from the Highlands of Scotland.

Roger closed his eyes and rubbed them. He opened his eyes. The dwarf was standing directly in front of him.

'Yes!' shouted Roger.

'Bellringers!' roared the dwarf. He began tugging at the clasp holding the flimsy cloak around his neck.

'Please,' said Roger, backing away. 'Don't . . .'

'Don't what?' asked the dwarf, still struggling with the clasp. 'I'm not going to do anything to you, ugly human. Get out of here.'

Roger turned to run.

'Wait!' The dwarf had stopped tugging and was now thumping the clasp with his stubby hands. 'What is your name?'

'I'm . . . Roger.'

'Strong name,' said the dwarf. 'Now go, Roger. And if you ever tell of this I'll come to your sleep room and eat you.'

Roger turned again.

'Wait!'

Roger stopped.

'Why were you dithering just now, and looking at your time dial?'

'I was going to the park,' said Roger, licking his lips. His mouth felt very dry. 'I've got to fight someone. But I'll go home instead. I promise.'

The dwarf stopped banging on the clasp and tilted his head to one side, looking closely at Roger.

'Fight, eh? Who you fight? You win fight? You are a good fighter, warrior?'

'Hugh . . . um, Hugh Ball,' said Roger. 'No, I won't win the fight. He's too big and I'm not a fighter. Actually, I should go home now.'

'No!' yelled the dwarf. 'Do not go home. Go fight Hughumhughball. Go now.'

Just as Roger turned to run, the dwarf banged the clasp – very hard – and vanished.

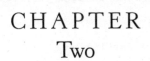

CHAPTER
Two

Roger ran, arms pumping, head down, round the corner and into the park entrance. A great cheer went up. Roger looked up and saw half the school standing in front of him. In the middle of the crowd was the hulking figure of Hugh Ball.

'Come on, Paxton,' yelled Hugh, thumping his fists together. 'I'm going to smash you for what you said to me. I am *not* a . . . umnittagated!'

Roger slowed to a halt. He stood, panting slightly, looking at the boy in front of him. Hugh was big. The two boys moved closer and began circling each other. The crowd fell silent.

Roger raised his fists, hands trembling and legs shaking.

Hugh stepped forward and swung a fist. Roger gasped and ducked. His legs buckled and he dropped to his knees. Directly in front of him was a large quivering stomach. He let fly with a punch. Hugh didn't even grunt as Roger's fist hit him and bounced off. Still kneeling, Roger felt a gust of wind as *something* flew past his head and struck Hugh's left foot. Glancing down, Roger could see a large dent in Hugh's shoe.

Roger stood up warily, the palms of his hands resting on his shaking thighs. He looked around. But there was no one else near them.

Hugh was standing absolutely still. His face was completely drained of colour, except for a small graze on the tip of his nose. His mouth was open and his eyes were wide with shock.

Roger raised his fists again.

'My foot . . .' said Hugh, pointing down at it.

Roger watched in amazement as Hugh hopped three times on his good foot, then toppled backwards and lay still.

The crowd went wild.

'Did you see that? I knew Roger would win.'

'That was karate, that was. Did you see the speed of that punch?'

'Fan-tas-tic. Knew Roger would beat him!'

Two of Hugh's followers rushed over and knelt beside him.

'Wh-what happened?' asked Roger, still shaking.

'You've killed him,' said Findlay McNuttal, looking up. 'That's what you've done with your . . . whatever you did.'

'But I didn't do that,' said Roger, pointing at the fallen figure.

'You did!' Martin Plumbly's voice screeched as he stood up and backed away. 'We all saw you. You hit poor Hugh so hard you've killed him.'

Hugh moaned, then his eyes blinked open and he began to cry.

'What's wrong with you?' asked Roger. 'And what happened to your nose?'

'My foot,' wailed Hugh, slowly sitting up. He reached out a hand and gingerly touched his hurt foot. 'You've broken it!' A tiny drop of blood from Hugh's grazed nose dropped on to his shirt. He put his hand up to his face and screamed.

'Oh be quiet!' shouted Roger, bending down and staring into Hugh's face.

Hugh stopped screaming.

Roger turned to walk away, then spun round again. 'And another thing,' he said, his voice almost a squeal. 'If I ever see you bullying *anyone* . . . I'll . . . I'll . . . I'll do something . . . *Understand?*'

Hugh nodded as tears ran down his face.

'Right, then,' squeaked Roger. 'That's . . .' He nodded his head and wagged a finger. 'That's . . . that, then . . . OK?'

'Yes,' sobbed Hugh.

'Good, good,' said Roger. 'That's good.' And he turned and made his way through the cheering, back-slapping crowd.

As he pushed away from the last of the well-wishers, Roger began to feel sick. He started to run. He ran into a narrow lane between some houses, stopped at a wall and bent over just as his stomach emptied.

'What a mess you make,' said a voice, puffing beside him. 'Why do you throw your food out?'

'Who's there?' asked Roger, wiping his mouth with the back of his hand and looking around. 'Where are you?'

'Here,' said the same voice, but now from in front.

'Not *again*,' said Roger. 'Go away, I don't want to see you.'

'Why not? I made you win the fight with Hughumhughball.'

The dwarf suddenly appeared in front of Roger. He was unclipping the flimsy cloak from its neck clasp.

'What did you do to Hugh?' asked Roger.

'Hit him with this,' said the dwarf, indicating his cudgel. 'Well, tried to hit him, but missed because you were in the way.'

Roger stopped wiping his mouth and watched as the

dwarf rolled up the cloak and slipped it into the satchel on his hip.

'If you'd struck his head you might have killed him,' said Roger. 'Your club nearly broke his nose. You skinned his nose! You broke his foot!'

'I am sorry,' said the dwarf. 'Next time I won't miss. I'll break his head for you.'

'No,' said Roger. 'You can't go around killing people.'

'You want to get a pummelling from Hughumhughball?'

'No,' said Roger. 'But you can't—'

'*Sheeesh!*' said the dwarf, raising a dirty, podgy finger to his lips. 'Did you hear a noise?'

'What noise?' Roger looked around anxiously. 'What?'

The dwarf did not answer. He spun round and pulled out his sword and axe. There was a soft *skittering* sound. Something dropped over the wall beside the dwarf.

Roger stared in horror as the thing approached. It was small with a smooth skull-shaped head and a wide grinning mouth. Its skin was a blotchy yellowish-grey, criss-crossed with tiny black pulsating veins. The creature had sunken eyes, a bent back and a forked tail. In its clawlike hands it held a crude wooden spear. The point of the spear was three rusty nails, bound with wire.

'What's . . . *that?*' gasped Roger, backing away rapidly.

'Gorefiend,' said the dwarf, moving forward, weapons swinging. 'Keep out of my way. I'll chop this smellsock into the smallest of pieces.'

'One moment,' said the gorefiend in a polite voice, as it sniffed the air around Roger. 'May I have the pleasure of introducing another of my friends?'

There was the same *skittering* noise and another armed gorefiend dropped over the wall.

'Oh,' said the first gorefiend, 'and more, if you please.'

Two more creatures dropped to the ground and moved towards the dwarf, waving their spears.

'Four, eh,' grunted the dwarf. 'Right, two for sword and two for axe. I'll cut off your heads and break your backs.'

Something caught the corner of Roger's eye. It was a fifth gorefiend, creeping over the wall behind the dwarf. It dropped to the ground and raised its spear above its head.

'Be-be-behind you!' Roger yelled, pointing a trembling finger.

The dwarf's sword arm slashed backwards and the blade caught the gorefiend in the chest just as it lunged forward with its spear. The spear missed the dwarf's back but plunged into his right leg.

'Front!' screeched Roger as the four remaining gorefiends attacked.

12

The dwarf threw his head back and bellowed, 'King Golmar's Braces!' as he limped forward with the spear still sticking out the back of his lower leg. He swung his axe, taking off the head of the first gorefiend.

'Oh,' said the head as it flew through the air. 'Thank you very much, I'm sure.'

A second gorefiend was dispatched with a sword lunge to the middle of its stomach. 'Nice one, Captain,' it said, as it fell. The third charged, its spear aimed at the dwarf's chest, and was killed by a sidestroke from the swinging axe. The remaining gorefiend threw its spear at the dwarf, who batted it easily to one side and hurled his axe in return. The axe just missed its target and clanged off the wall. The gorefiend sniffed several times then, cackling madly, it scrambled over the wall and vanished.

'Festering fustilugs,' snarled the dwarf, sheathing his sword and limping over to retrieve his axe. 'I should not have missed that one. Come here, Roger. Help me with my leg.'

Roger took a couple of steps. The remains of the four gorefiends began to smoke and spark; yellow gunge bubbled out as flames quickly consumed their bodies. In seconds all that remained was a faint yellow tinge on the ground and an unpleasant aroma. Roger began to feel queasy again.

'Hurry,' said the dwarf. 'There may be more. Quickly. Pull this out.'

'I c-can't,' said Roger, backing away and covering his eyes.

'Do it!' snapped the dwarf, shaking his fist. 'Or I'll let your brains out of your head.'

Roger moved towards the dwarf and took hold of the small spear. He closed his eyes and looked away.

'Now,' the dwarf spoke softly, 'when I say pull, pull as hard as you can. Understand me?'

Roger nodded, his eyes still tightly shut.

'Pull!'

Roger yanked at the spear with all of his strength. There was a slight sucking noise as the spear came free. His arms flew up over his head and he stumbled back into the wall behind him. As he hit the rough stone, he felt the spear he was holding plunge into something soft.

Someone screamed.

Roger let go of the spear and turned round. The spear was sticking in the thigh of a snarling, red-eyed dwarf standing on top of the wall. The dwarf was wobbling violently and waving an axe. Roger reached out and grabbed the corner of the dwarf's wildly flapping cloak. The dwarf steadied himself, and then swung his axe. Roger ducked as the axe whistled over his head and down, cutting through the cloak he was holding. Screaming again, the dwarf toppled backwards. There was a loud thump, a torrent of jumbled words from the dwarf, followed by several *skittering* sounds, and then silence.

'I knew that blustering whiteliver would be skulking nearby,' shouted the first dwarf. 'The cowardly trundletail would not eyeball me in nose-to-nose combat.' He made a low moan of pain. 'However, my judgement is, as usual, as sound as a badger's belch. I have been searching for a worthy warrior to carry out an act of noble insanity, to face almost certain death. And you are indeed such a warrior! You have no fear in challenging stronger enemies like Hughumhughball. And now you have wounded Leatherhead Barnstorm and attacked him with your bare hands.' The dwarf gave another moan of pain, followed by a chuckle. 'That gave my wink-a-peeps great pleasure.' His voice grew deeper. 'You are the one. I choose you for my Destroyer. So named, so be it.'

'Wh-wh-wh . . .' Roger stared back at the wall. He looked at the piece of material in his hand and then at the wall again. 'Wh-what happened? Who *was* that? What did he say?'

'Ah, nothing, just a death curse.'

'What?' Roger dropped the bit of cloak and pointed at the empty wall. 'What do you mean?'

'Do not concern yourself with it. It's a simple description of how he will kill you. How many days he will take and the variety of methods he would employ to ensure maximum suffering. That is all.'

'I didn't . . .' Roger could barely speak. 'I pulled it out – it just – I didn't mean to – should I go and look for him?'

'Ah, you want to go after him and kill him!' said the dwarf. 'Spoken like a true warrior. No, he is long gone. Come to me, I need your assistance.'

Roger blinked his eyes several times and went over to the dwarf.

He was sitting on the ground, unfolding a large red handkerchief. He wound it around his leg, pulled it tight and knotted it firmly. The dwarf stood up and stamped his foot, only to give a little shriek of pain and sit down again.

Roger knelt beside him. 'Is there anything I can do?'

'Yes,' said the dwarf, groaning and holding his leg. 'Very sore leg. Must get away from here. Can you get a wheeled carriage to remove me?'

'A what?' asked Roger.

'Wheeled carriage. A carriage with wheels, to put me in. I cannot walk far like this.'

'Oh,' said Roger, looking around. 'Right, hang on, I'll see what I can do.'

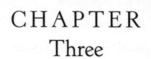

CHAPTER
Three

Roger left the dwarf sitting on the ground and ran out of the lane. There was nothing on his side of the road but houses. Across the road was a general store with two empty pushchairs sitting outside the entrance.

Roger crossed the road, grabbed the sturdier-looking of the two pushchairs and wheeled it back to the waiting dwarf.

'Good, Roger,' said the dwarf. 'You steal the carriage?'

'Um . . . borrowed,' said Roger.

'Help me in,' said the dwarf, scooping up some small bits of gravel in his hand.

Roger helped the surprisingly heavy little man get to his feet and then gently settled him into the pushchair.

'I'll take you home,' said Roger. 'My mum's a nurse. She'll know what to do with your leg.'

'First,' said the dwarf, 'give this to the carriage owner.' He held out his fist and dropped several small golden nuggets into Roger's hand. 'Then we must find the Witchwatcher of Auchterbolton.'

'Is that . . . gold?' asked Roger. 'How did—?'

'Go give, quickly,' growled the dwarf. 'We must leave.'

Roger dodged traffic as he ran back across the road. A puzzled-looking woman holding a toddler by the hand was standing outside the shop; a large shopping bag lay at her feet.

'You lost your pushchair?' asked Roger.

The woman nodded.

'Me and a dwarf have borrowed it,' said Roger, holding out his hand with the golden nuggets. 'He's been injured by a gorefiend stabbing him in the leg with a spear. We need to get away quickly. So we're sorry, but you can buy another buggy with this.'

The woman's mouth fell open as Roger dropped the gold into her palm.

'Oh,' said Roger, looking into the woman's eyes. 'And he killed four gorefiends – they smell awful – and now he wants to find a . . . a Witchwatcher.' He licked his lips as he thought about what he had just said. 'What do you think I should do?' he whispered, staring intently at the woman.

There was no reply. The woman bit her bottom lip and pulled the toddler closer.

'The gorefiends burn up all yellow,' Roger continued. 'And I-I did something really bad with a spear. It was an accident. I didn't mean to . . .'

The woman shook her head. Her mouth opened and closed silently. The toddler tugged at her hand, then kicked over the shopping bag, spilling its contents on the pavement.

Roger took a deep breath, gave a little shudder, and turned to cross the road again. 'OK, thanks anyway. Sorry about your pushchair. Nice wee boy you've got.'

'She's a girl,' said the woman, finding her voice at last.

'Right,' said Roger, and he dashed back over the road, leaving the woman still standing in the same position.

'Onwards, Roger,' said the dwarf as Roger returned. 'Now we go find the Witchwatcher Gwendolena Goodroom, and make our stand against the dark forces.'

'No,' said Roger, pulling out a tartan blanket lying folded in the bottom carry-tray of the pushchair. 'We're going to my house.' He began to cover the dwarf's head and body with the blanket.

'What are you doing?' grumbled the dwarf. 'Waylay this frippery. We *must* go find Goodroom the Witchwatcher. It is urgent!'

'Now, look!' Roger shouted. 'I've had enough. I don't know who or what you are. You suddenly appear and

19

nearly kill Hugh. You appear again and kill gore-things. And I do something . . . horrible. I'm not doing any more. I'm going home, and if you want to come with me, my mum will help you. If not, then just stay here. I'm off.' Roger turned and began to walk away.

The dwarf grunted. 'Stay, Roger. Wait.'

Roger looked back at the tartan-covered figure almost hidden in the pushchair.

'We'll go see your maternal human,' said the dwarf. 'I need to stop the bleeding and weaken the pain.'

Roger walked back to the pushchair. He tucked away some beard hair sticking out of the blanket and then got behind the chair to push it out of the lane.

'We'll go this way,' said Roger. 'Keep that cover pulled up as far as you can so people can't see your face, so they don't see that you're a . . . that you're different. And tuck your beard in.'

The dwarf grunted, but did as he was told.

Roger tried to avoid people as he pushed the dwarf through the streets. Everything went well until he turned into the road where he lived and walked straight into two of his neighbours: Agnes McKeek and Anna Botting.

'Well, well, Agnes,' said Mrs Botting, breaking off her conversation. 'Look what we have here. The Paxton boy has got himself a baby. Did your father bring that back from the oil rigs, or is he still away, working overtime, eh?'

The two women giggled, snorting and pushing at each other.

'No,' said Roger quietly. 'My dad's not home just now.'

'Whose is it?' asked Mrs McKeek. 'It's too big to be very new.'

Both women moved towards Roger. Roger took a couple of backward steps, pulling the pushchair with him.

'Don't move, Roger Paxton,' snapped Mrs Botting.

'Stay right where you are,' said Mrs McKeek. 'Let's have a look at this child.'

'I can explain,' began Roger. 'It's not what it looks like.'

Mrs Botting and Mrs McKeek leaned right into the pushchair and slowly pulled down the tartan cover.

'Oh, in the name of . . . !' Mrs Botting spoke in a shocked whisper.

'It's a monster!' gasped Mrs McKeek.

The dwarf pushed himself upright on his good leg and shook a gleaming axe at the women. '*Kirkiemachough, you blob-tailed buttermilks!*' he bellowed at the top of his voice.

21

Mrs McKeek screamed, dropped her shopping bag, and ran across the road, waving her arms in the air. She tripped over the edge of the pavement, pirouetted gracefully, and fell backwards through a small privet hedge. There was a loud *ooof* as she hit the ground. She lay on her back, gasping and whimpering, her legs sticking out of the hedge.

Mrs Botting started running, both hands over her mouth to control a sudden attack of hiccups. She reached the pavement on the far side of the road, jumped over Mrs Botting in the hedge and, without a backward glance, ran across the front garden and disappeared round the side of the house.

'Help, Anna, help,' gasped Mrs McKeek, as her friend vanished. 'I can't . . . hardly breathe.'

At that very second a police car came hurtling round the corner. Two policemen were in the front, and in the back was a woman Roger recognised as Hugh Ball's mother. The car pulled up outside Roger's house and both policemen jumped out, ran up the path and started hammering on the front door.

The door opened and Roger's mother appeared, holding his little sister.

Roger started to back away, but just then Mrs Ball spotted him. 'That's him there, the hooligan,' she yelled, pointing at Roger and struggling to get out of the police car. 'That's the bully who nearly killed my poor wee Hughie.'

'Rod-ger!' Roger's sister, Hannah, shouted and waved at her brother while his mother stood looking bewildered.

'Come play with me, Rod-ger,' yelled Hannah.

The policemen left Mrs Paxton and began to sprint down the road towards Roger.

At that moment Mrs Ball sprang out of the police car and staggered on to the pavement, waving a large handbag around her head. 'Get him!' she screamed. 'Get the wee—'

The running policemen collided with the screaming woman and her large handbag. All three crashed to the ground. One of the policemen was trapped under Mrs Ball; he appeared to be unconscious.

The other policeman got to his feet and took a few wobbly steps before tripping over Mrs McKeek's legs dangling from the hedge.

Roger, on the other side of the road, looked at his mother and sister for a moment. Then he turned the pushchair round and began to run.

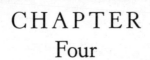

CHAPTER
Four

'What've you done?' howled Roger, as he ran. 'Everyone's after me. They'll put me in jail.'

'Move quickly,' said the dwarf. 'I think the protectors of your peace are annoyed. You may be taken captive.'

Roger kept going. He was a good runner, but the pushchair was heavy and his arms and legs were beginning to ache. Just ahead was the entrance to a supermarket. Roger wrestled the pushchair round a corner and sideswiped a shopping trolley being pushed by an elderly couple. Some of the shopping on the elderly couple's trolley fell off.

Roger kept running.

'*You stupid eejit!*' yelled the old man.

'Sorry,' panted Roger, looking back just in time to see the old woman throwing a can at him.

The can whizzed past his head and smashed through the side window of a car driving out of the car park. The old woman bent down and picked up a grapefruit. She swung it overarm and let fly. Roger ducked. The grapefruit hit the face of the driver who was getting out of the car with the broken window.

'Oi, you!'

Roger looked beyond the old woman and saw that one of the policemen had appeared.

'You're under arrest,' roared the policeman, stabbing his finger at Roger in a furious manner.

'*What, me?*' The old woman stood up, turned round, and threw a small bulky bag at the policeman. 'I'll under-arrest-you. Go and catch some proper criminals.'

The bag scored a direct hit on the policeman's chest. Flour exploded everywhere.

Roger shoved the pushchair off the pavement and ran through the car park, past the main supermarket entrance and round a corner. People shouted as he swerved around them, and several dogs tied up outside the automatic doors began to bark.

He ran down the side of the supermarket until he reached an open gate with a notice that read: UNLOADING BAY – KEEP CLEAR. Beyond the gate was a closed roller-door with a white van parked beside it. He was in a dead end!

The dwarf pulled back the tartan cover, threw it on the ground and then gingerly stepped out of the pushchair and limped over to the wall beside the roller-door. He stood with his back pressed against the wall.

'Come,' said the dwarf, fumbling in his satchel. 'Hurry.'

Roger let go of the chair and ran over. The dwarf grabbed Roger's arms and turned him around.

'Kneel down,' said the dwarf.

Roger did so. There was a moment's pause and then the flimsy material of a cloak enveloped him.

'Work,' muttered the dwarf, pulling the hood over his head.

Roger heard a click.

'Do not move,' said the dwarf, 'and control noisy breathing.'

'Sorry,' said Roger, trying to stop his panting.

'*Sheeesh!*' said the dwarf.

Roger fell silent. His knees were sore now. He heard footsteps and voices.

'I can see through this,' whispered Roger. 'I can see everything. Can they see me?'

'I am not certain,' answered the dwarf. Then he rapped his knuckles on Roger's head. 'You'll have your answer soon. Now keep your mouth quiet.'

A policeman, followed by two supermarket security guards, walked round the corner. The policeman was covered in flour, and Roger could see that the officer's trousers were ripped at the side and his shirt was sticking through the tear.

'There's the pushchair,' said a guard, pointing.

'And what have we got here?' said the policeman, looking at the crumpled tartan blanket lying on the ground.

Roger tried to stand, but the dwarf pulled him down.

'Got you!' said the policeman, stretching out a hand.

Roger closed his eyes.

CHAPTER
Five

'Blast,' said the policeman, holding up the tartan blanket. 'I thought he was hiding under this.' He threw the blanket on the ground beside the van and began to hammer on the roller-door with the side of his fist. 'Open up, I know you're in there. Open up, this is the law.'

There was a muffled shout from inside and the door began to roll upwards. A thin, scruffy man with tattooed arms appeared, followed by two men wearing supermarket uniforms.

'What's all your noise?' asked the tattooed man, beginning to grin as he looked at the policeman. 'Have you been baking a cake, sonny?'

'We're looking for a boy and an . . . individual of restricted height. Did they come in here?'

'Naw, just me and my boxes. There's naebody else in here, not in the last twenty minutes anyhow.' The tattooed man turned to the two men behind him. 'Have they?'

The men shook their heads. 'What's he done?' asked

one of the men. 'This boy and . . . the individual of restricted height?'

'Everything,' said the policeman, looking around the inside of the building. 'Serious assault, breaking toes, pushing women through hedges, damaging cars, you name it and he's done it.' He pointed to the rip in his trousers. 'Police assault. My partner as well, knocked him out.'

'Some boy,' said the tattooed man. 'And what's this restricted-height individual person?'

'I don't rightly know,' said the policeman, coming back out of the building. 'It might be another boy, although from the hairiness, it could be a monkey or some sort of monster.'

The men began to chortle.

'Did this . . .' the tattooed man spluttered, 'monkey-monster tear yer trousers, mister, and throw powder at you?'

'It's not funny.' The policeman glared at the tattooed man. 'Any more of that and I'll arrest *you*.'

'Sorry,' giggled the tattooed man, barely able to control himself.

'Right, then . . .' said the policeman. 'Come on, you two.' He pointed at the two security guards. 'Let's go back and sort out the two old numpties in the car park.'

As the policeman and the guards reached the corner,

Roger slowly stood up. *'Follow me,'* he whispered to the dwarf. *'Don't make a noise.'*

He and the dwarf shuffled silently towards the back of the van.

The tattooed man, still laughing, shouted after the policeman. 'Hope there's no more monkey business, officer.'

'Yer an awfy man, Wullie,' laughed one of the supermarket men.

'Ah hope he never heard you,' said the other.

'I'm no caring,' said Wullie. 'I'm away on the rest of my deliveries. Fasten the back doors for me, will yuh?'

Wullie climbed into the driver's seat of his van and started the engine. He waited until there were two loud bangs from the back before driving off. Wullie waved at the men as his van turned the corner.

When he'd gone, one of the supermarket men scratched his head. 'That's funny,' he said.

'What is?' asked the other.

'That blanket.'

'Aye, what about it?'

'It's gone.'

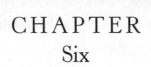

CHAPTER
Six

'That was good brain-thinking,' said the dwarf, trying to steady himself in the back of the swaying van. 'You are a quick-witter. But must this carriage pull and push?'

'Sit down,' said Roger. 'Jam yourself against the boxes and you'll be all right.'

The dwarf carefully lowered himself to the floor of the van.

Roger looked around. As far as he could see, the van was half full of cardboard boxes all containing the same brand of paper towels.

'Are you OK?' he asked, as the dwarf gingerly stretched out his wounded leg on top of the tartan blanket.

'Yes. Forget my leg limb. Where is this carriage taking us?'

'I don't know,' said Roger. 'I only got in here to get away from that policeman.'

'Now hear me,' said the dwarf. 'We must proceed with all haste to Auchterbolton. No delay is acceptable.'

'What do you mean, "we"?' asked Roger. 'I'm only here by accident. I don't even know who you are.'

The dwarf glared at Roger. 'I am Mossbelly MacFearsome, Captain of the Royal Guard. Protector of Queen Gwri, the rightful heir to King Golmar, Ruler of the Innerland.'

'I . . . don't know what you are talking about,' said Roger slowly. 'You just suddenly appeared and started killing things.' He shook his head. 'I've no idea what's happening, or what you're talking about.'

Mossbelly MacFearsome gripped his axe and bent forward. 'And you are a disrespectful ugly human. Do not talk to me in that voice or I'll cut out your insides and place them on your outsides.'

'Oh, just . . .' said Roger, lying back against the boxes. He folded his arms across his chest.

The van swung hard right. Some boxes fell over. One landed on the dwarf's wounded leg. He groaned and knocked the box aside as the van began to accelerate.

Roger and the dwarf sat in silence, not looking at each other.

After a while the van began to slow down. It turned left, bumped over something metallic-sounding, and stopped.

'Quick,' said Roger. 'Up there.' He pointed at the piled-up boxes.

The dwarf got to his feet and, with Roger's help, climbed over the pile and into a narrow space at the top.

Roger made sure the dwarf was hidden, then followed him up and pulled two boxes in front of them, leaving only a small gap to see through.

A door slammed, and seconds later the back doors of the van opened. Roger watched as Wullie lifted out some boxes and, whistling tunelessly, disappeared from sight.

'Now,' hissed Roger. 'Let's get out of here.'

Roger and the dwarf pushed the boxes aside and climbed down. Roger peered around the open doors. They were in a service station area with a café and some shops. Wullie was just entering one of them.

Roger picked up the tartan blanket and jumped out of the van. He turned round and held out both hands to help the dwarf. The little man grasped Roger's hands in his knobbly fists and leaned forward. The weight was more than Roger could bear and the two of them crashed to the ground.

Roger stood up quickly. Mossbelly MacFearsome lay on the ground, moaning.

'You all right?' asked Roger, anxiously looking around. 'Sorry about that. We'll need to get away before we're seen.'

The dwarf got to his feet. Roger took his arm and they made their way around the side of the van. They hobbled past the café, ducking under the windows. A baby in a highchair smiled at them and smacked a rattle against a window. The baby's parents were busy eating and did not look up. Roger and the dwarf reached the back of the café. They clambered over a small fence and slithered down a steep embankment. At the bottom of the embankment they lay on their backs, breathing deeply.

'Well done, Roger,' said the dwarf, after a few moments. 'You are indeed an admirable companion for a great undertaking. I say sorry for being crumpsy with you. And you can use the diminutive of my first name. Call me Moss.'

Roger turned his head to look at the dwarf. 'OK, Moss. But – ' he shook his head – 'I haven't done anything.'

'Oh but you have, modest ugly human. You have been of immense help in this quest.'

'What? What have I done?'

'Did you not see the great sign?'

Roger frowned. 'What are you talking about? What sign?'

'Go and look.' Moss chuckled. 'Look to the north.

You will see the sign. Go.' He pointed back up the embankment.

Roger scrambled up the grass on all fours. At the top he looked around. All he could see was the main carriageway with the evening rush-hour cars whizzing in both directions. Then he saw it. At the exit from the service area was a road sign indicating the A9 road to Inverness, Pitlochry and Dunkeld. But it was the first name on the board that held his attention: *Auchterbolton.*

And it was only five miles away.

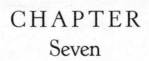

CHAPTER
Seven

Roger slid back down the embankment. 'I saw it,' he said, sitting down beside the dwarf. 'It's not far, you could walk it. It wouldn't take you too long.'

'Not with this leg limb,' said Moss. 'The leaking and pain must be fixed before we travel to Auchterbolton.' He pointed to a field in the distance. 'Do you see that cultivation with the forest beyond?'

Roger nodded. 'Yes . . .'

'We shall hide in the woodland during the darkness hours and mend my leg limb.'

'All night?' Roger shook his head. 'I can't do that. I need to go home.'

'Listen,' said Moss, staring intently at Roger. 'We are on a quest. We *must* continue until we succeed – or die. The ogres must *not* be allowed to rise. It is too soon. Do you understand my words?'

'Ye-s,' said Roger, his voice breaking a little. 'But I still want to go home tonight.'

'Roger.' Moss leaned closer. 'Help me, and I'll make things better. When we complete our quest, your difficulties will all be sorted. You will be rewarded. I promise.'

'Really?' Roger sniffed loudly and pulled back from the face gazing intently at him.

The dwarf nodded. 'Trust me.'

Roger bent his head, picked at some blades of grass and thought about what had happened to him since he had met the dwarf. There was no believable story that he could possibly tell anyone.

'All right, I'll help,' he said, looking up after a few moments. 'But just remember I'm not a brave warrior. And I *must* phone my mum, let her know I'm safe.'

'You have a speak-hear box with you?' asked Moss.

'No,' said Roger, as he understood what the dwarf was asking. 'We're not allowed them at school. Maybe I can use a phone in the café up there.'

'Go quickly,' said Moss. 'Do not get snared by humans.'

Roger began to climb up the embankment again. Halfway up, he stopped and looked back. 'What if we don't succeed with this quest? What happens to me then?'

Moss laughed. 'Then our troubles will be greater than your worst nocturnal dreams. Go. Quickly.'

When Roger returned, Moss was picking at wildflowers, easing up their roots with his dagger and then placing them in his satchel.

'Did you speak with your maternal one?' asked Moss, closing his satchel.

Roger just nodded and sat down.

'What's wrong, Roger? You are looking mubblefubbled.'

'Nothing,' said Roger, pulling at some grass.

Moss stood up and limped over to Roger. He put a hand under his chin and lifted his face. 'Tell it to me. I need to know.'

'It's my mum,' said Roger. 'She's upset, crying on the phone. She thinks I've run away. Because of the fight with Hugh, and the police coming round. She's got enough trouble with my dad being away all the time. She wants me home.'

'What did you say to her?' asked Moss.

'I said I was helping a friend and that I would be home soon; that everything was a misunderstanding and that I would explain later. But she just cried.'

'Listen to my words, Roger. I have made you a promise – as binding as an oath! Dwarves *keep* promises, unlike the human race. Things will be made better for you. Now come, we must hide in that woodland until the new day.'

Roger got to his feet. To his surprise the dwarf took his hand and kept hold of it until they reached the edge of the field.

'We cross this abomination,' said Moss. 'Then we'll be in a safer place. Help me through this keep-out.'

Roger pulled apart the loose fence wires to let the dwarf duck through. 'It's just a field,' he said, as he followed Moss.

'Just a-a field!' spluttered Moss. He cleared his throat and spat on the ground. 'It's an *agri-culture* is what it is. You ever tried living under one? The noise – digging, clanking, banging. Should not be allowed. Near as bad as church bells a-boinging through the earth until a dwarf's teeth are screaming.'

Roger did not answer as he and Moss made their way over the ploughed field to a wooden fence at the far side.

'What now?' asked Roger, looking beyond the fence to the thickly wooded area. 'We'll need to get you over this. It'll be difficult to climb with your leg.'

'Follow me,' said Moss, unsheathing his axe and limping forward.

Before Roger could say anything, Moss raised his axe and smashed a section of the fence to pieces; then, still holding his axe, the dwarf walked into the forest. 'Hurry up,' he growled as he disappeared round a tree. 'Don't be a slitherum.'

Roger stepped over the broken fence and followed.

Despite his wound, Moss moved quickly. He made no effort to slow down, ducking under branches and climbing over fallen trees. After walking for several minutes Moss stopped in a small clearing and stared up at the sky. He looked at the setting sun, then knelt down and placed the right side of his head on the ground.

'Here,' said Moss, standing again with some difficulty. 'We remain here for the night.'

'Would it not be better if we had a bit more space?' asked Roger, looking around.

'This is fine,' said Moss, pulling his satchel over his head. 'We spend our night hours in this spinkie-den. Now fetch fallen wood while I begin to heal wound.'

'What kind of wood do you want?' said Roger.

'Fallen wood only.' Moss sat down and began rummaging through his satchel. He waved a hand dismissively at Roger. 'Go.'

Roger glared at the dwarf for a moment before turning away.

There was plenty of wood lying around. Roger gathered as much as he could carry. When he returned Moss was working on his leg. Roger dropped the wood on the ground and stood watching the dwarf.

'More,' said Moss through gritted teeth. 'More wood. Go.'

Four more times Roger gathered wood and returned with it to the dwarf. On the fifth time Moss held up his hand. 'Enough. That's enough.'

Roger put down the wood and looked at Moss's leg. The trouser leg was rolled up above the knee and the wound was covered in a foul-looking mixture of mud, flowers and ferns.

'Are you OK?' Roger grimaced as he gazed at the knobbly limb. 'Can I help?'

'Yes,' said Moss, holding out his red handkerchief. 'Help tie this snotter-clout around and in a firm knot.'

Roger knelt and wrapped the handkerchief around the caked mixture. Before pulling the knot tight, he held both pointed ends in his hands and looked into Moss's face.

'Now,' said Moss. 'Pull tight, *slowly*. And stop when I tell you.'

Roger crossed the ends and began to pull.

'Stop,' gasped Moss, his face screwed up in pain. 'Tie. Tie fast.'

Roger quickly tied the ends in a reef knot.

'Good.' Moss leaned back and rested his head against a tree. 'Now we wait until the pain ebbs and my strength returns.'

'How about the wood?' asked Roger, nodding at the pile lying on the ground. 'Do you want to start a fire?'

'No. No fire. Smoke could be seen.'

'What's all the wood for, then? Do you want me to build something?'

'Not for anything.' Moss began chuckling. 'Keeps forest clean. I don't like a messy forest.' The little man shook with laughter and then closed his eyes. Within seconds he had begun to snore.

Roger stood looking at the snoring dwarf. For a moment it crossed his mind that he should walk away and try to get home. But he had made an agreement. He sat down next to Moss, glanced at his watch and then closed his eyes.

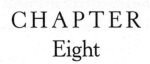

CHAPTER
Eight

'Healing is taking place.'

Roger jerked awake. Moss was on his feet stretching his hands above his head. Roger looked at his watch; he had been asleep for about thirty minutes.

'Your leg can't be better,' said Roger. 'It would take a lot longer than that to heal.'

'Not healed,' said Moss, pulling out his sword and axe. 'Healing. Be a lot better on the morrow. Come, there are things to do before we feed and sleep.'

'What?' asked Roger, getting to his feet.

'First, stretch.' Moss lifted his arms above his head. 'Then fetch more wood. I have a joke with you before, but we need wood to make a protection barricade.'

Roger stretched, hands reaching skywards and standing on his tiptoes.

'Good,' said Moss. 'Always start with a stretch. Keeps body supple. Now, more wood. Go.'

Roger began to collect wood. He could hear chopping noises coming from the direction of the dwarf.

With each load of wood Roger brought back he could see that Moss was constructing a small circular barricade. The dwarf was working at a furious pace, cutting the wood into roughly equal lengths and then hammering them into the ground with the flat of his axe. With the circle almost complete, Moss started cutting leafy branches from the surrounding trees. He placed some of them on the inside of the barricade and others he laid over part of the top to serve as a roof.

'That's clever,' said Roger, dropping another load of wood. 'Do you want any more?'

'No more.' Moss indicated a large flat stone. 'Carry that inside for a table.'

Roger lifted the stone and placed it in the middle of the construction. 'Now sit,' said Moss, completing the circle of the barricade, then sheathing his sword and axe and sitting down himself.

Roger sat beside the stone and crossed his legs. The branches he was sitting on were springy and surprisingly comfortable.

'Are you hungry?' Moss asked, rummaging in his satchel. 'You throw your last meal away after fighting with Hughumhughball.'

'I don't know,' said Roger. 'I haven't thought about—'
His stomach rumbled.

'Ah, I hear that you are!' said Moss, taking out
his dagger. 'You need bellyfuel. I'll cut you a slice
of pie.'

Moss carefully lifted a cloth bundle out of the satchel
and laid it on top of the stone. He unwrapped the cloth to
reveal a large crusty pie.

Roger's stomach rumbled again.

'Just a moment, hungry belly,' said Moss as he cut the
pie in two and handed one piece to Roger.

'Thank you,' said Roger. 'I *am* hungry.'

'Eat,' said Moss, taking a large bite out of his pie.
Pastry crumbs dropped into his beard where they mingled
with previous droppings.

Roger held up his pie and sniffed; the smell was
delicious. He took a bite; the taste was delicious. It was
tangy and sweet. It was soft and it was crunchy. It was the
best pie he had ever tasted.

'This is lovely,' said Roger.

'Merry-go-down?' Moss held out a small rounded
bottle with a cork stopper.

Roger took the bottle and watched as Moss pulled an
identical bottle from his satchel and tugged out the
stopper with his teeth. Roger did the same. Moss took a

large gulp, wiped his mouth with the back of his hand and said: *'Aaaahhh.'*

Roger raised his bottle and took a long swallow. He put his hand up to wipe his mouth; there was a warm glow spreading all the way through his body. He took another drink.

'That's nice as well,' he said. 'Like raspberries an' grapes.' He gave a little laugh. 'And ish sweet.'

'Finish your pie,' said Moss. 'No more until you finish pie. Then just a nipperkin.'

'I'll finish it,' giggled Roger, starting to feel a bit woozy. 'Don't you worry about that, Mossy. I'll eat your pie. What kinda pie issit?'

'Mushworm.'

Roger gave Moss a huge smile. 'Mushworm! That's a great one. I like that. Good joke.' He giggled and took another drink from the bottle. 'Now, Mossy, I want to ask you a few queshions about every . . . everything.' Roger waved his hands about before stuffing more pie into his mouth. He lifted the bottle, but before he could drink again the dwarf leaned over and snatched it out of his hand.

'No more.' Moss had a stern look on his face. 'I forget human age. A dwarf is fully growed at three years and greybeard at seven. Ask questions. I'll tell you what you want to know about our quest.'

46

'You're an old sport-spoil,' said Roger, settling back, leaning against the wooden barricade. He felt great: warm, comfortable, very clear-headed and extremely happy. 'Tell me *everything*,' he said, putting the last of the pie into his mouth. 'Miss nothing out. I want to know what you're doing here, where you come from and what we're going to do next. Tell all, Mossy-boy, OK?'

Mossbelly MacFearsome picked at his teeth with the point of his dagger, then took another swallow from his bottle. He burped, and began to tell his story.

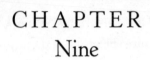

CHAPTER
Nine

'Long ago,' said Moss, 'many different creatures lived on Earth. They all lived in peace, more or less, except for humans. They were newest race and most troublesome. Humans liked to rule, to dominate. They quarrelled with everyone, and had no regard for nature or anything earthborn but themselves.'

Moss took another drink from his bottle as Roger gazed wide-eyed at him.

'A great gathering was called to decide the fate of the human race. Many wanted to put an end to the troublesome creatures, to destroy them completely.'

Roger, head swaying slightly, leaned forward. 'Did they do it?'

Moss narrowed his eyes and tilted his head. 'Think you'd be here if the human race had been destroyed?'

'Oh, no,' said Roger. 'That wash silly of me. I wouldn't be here, would I? What happened? Why'm I still here?'

'The dwarves. The dwarves saved you, my ugly friend.

They spoke for your survival. They said you were a young, stupid race and that it would be wrong to destroy you without giving you time to mature and that they would fight to defend humans.'

Moss drained his bottle and reached for the other one.

'For a time, war came near. But after a period of sensible thought, a compromise was agreed to save the ugly ones.'

'What?' said Roger, grinning happily.

'For an allotted period of time, dwarves would dwell in their underground halls and ogres would slumber in the earth. The upper world would be left mainly to humans. The humans promised to mend their ways, if they were given sufficient time. And if they succeeded, all would live together. But if they *failed*, they would be destroyed by the combined might of dwarves, ogres and others united against them. Watchers would report on the making of progress and the humans' treatment of the world.'

'I don't undershtand,' said Roger. 'Where are all these ogres now? And how long did the humans get to prove themselves?'

Moss took another swallow before answering.

'The ogres are under the Earth's surface, their resting places marked by standing stones. They'll sleep until the allotted time – or if the Doomstone Sword awakens them, if it should prove *necessary*, if we cannot *afford* to wait the time agreed, due to human behaviour. Humans have only one hundred and thirty-seven years left to prove worthy. The reports are not good. They – *you* and your kind – have forgotten their promise. Humans spoil the earth, the sea and the sky. They wage war and have come close to destroying the Earth ball.'

'You're doing it again,' said Roger. 'You're answering questions with answers that I don't undershtand. What's . . . the Doomstone Sword?'

'The Doomstone Sword,' said Moss sternly, 'was created by the greatest wizards from all the lands above and below earth and sea. Named as such, for only this sword can strike the stones and awaken the ogres early – and bring doom upon the human race. It was made from siderite fallen from the sky, mixed with ferromagnetic agate and infused with a most powerful magic spell. Then it was tempered by fire and beaten continually for seventeen days and eighteen nights. Finally it was hardened in dragon's breath. All creatures of this world, except humans, can feel its power. Whomsoever holds the sword in his hand must be obeyed. No dwarf can resist. We cannot attack or harm the holder of the sword; its power over us is absolute. When it is encased in stone or beneath water, the spell is benevolent; our sense of it is peaceful. But if it is unleashed its power is great.'

'Wow!' said Roger, grinning madly. He gave a small hiccup.

'And this . . .' Moss rummaged in his satchel and pulled out a small black hammer with a gold band just below the head. 'This is the only thing that can stop it. This was created at the same time as the Doomstone Sword and with the same materials. But in addition it has a small piece of obsidian and a destruction spell. It's the only thing that can break the sword and drain its power.'

'Wow, again!' said Roger. 'What's it called?'

'A hammer.'

'That's not fair,' said Roger. 'It should have a proper name, like the Doomstone Sword. It should be the Mighty Hammer of Smiting and Doom-Dealing Destruction.'

Moss sniffed. 'I'd say it's *the* hammer, but . . .' He leaned closer and shook the hammer at Roger. With the fingers of his other hand he tapped the side of his nose, twice. Then he pushed his beard slightly to one side and gently patted the plain black hammer that was strapped to his chest. 'Do you understand what I say when I give you the two-nose tap and tell you that this –' he waggled the hammer with the gold band under Roger's nose – 'is a *hammer*? But this –' he placed his other hand against the hammer on his chest – 'is the *true* hammer? The one I'll give to you when the time has come?'

51

'*Tee-hee-hee.*' Roger giggled, tapped the side of his own nose twice. 'I do, I do too, so I do-do.'

'Exactly!' shouted Moss, giving a large wink. 'Now you know!'

Roger giggled again and winked back. But he was having a little difficulty concentrating on what Moss was saying. And his head had started to move about by itself.

'I do not lie to you,' said Moss, still waggling the hammer in his hand. 'You have the truth, but –' the dwarf grinned and pointed at his chest, then held up two stubby fingers and again tapped them twice on the side of his nose – 'only one is true.' He nodded and gave a low rumbling laugh.

Roger hiccupped. He really had no idea what Moss was talking about. It was all just nonsense. But he was having fun for the first time since he had bumped into the dwarf, and he had just thought of an *absolutely-brilliantly-funny* reply. He giggled to himself, then pursed his lips and tried to look serious. 'I unershtand!' he said. *This was going to be hilarious.* Then he shouted, '*You've got two noses!*'

There was a pause, and both of them burst out laughing. Moss's laugh was like cannonballs rolling down a tin roof.

'Good jocularity,' said Moss, wheezing a little and

52

wiping his eyes. 'Warriors enjoy joking with each other. It is a dwarvely thing to do.'

'That *was* great,' said Roger, grinning foolishly. 'I enjoyed that. Now, where's the Doomstone Sword? I like the sound of . . . this sword. Do you . . . *hic* . . . do you know where it ish?'

Moss nodded. 'Long ago the Doomstone Sword was set in stone and left for the human race as a remembrance that they were on trial. But a powerful magician freed the sword. In the wrong hands it caused death and destruction until a human threw the sword into a lake.' Moss slipped the hammer into his satchel. 'The sword remained in the water realm throughout the centuries, mostly forgotten. Leatherhead Barnstorm has been searching for it for years, and now he has found it, in a lake in the country of England. The human race now faces extinction, before their allotted time. Perhaps no time is left.'

'Wait-wait-wait,' spluttered Roger. 'Whassa Leatherfred Bumstrom?' He waved a hand at the dwarf, then stopped and yawned. 'Sorry, I'm getting . . . very sleepy. Explain, please.'

'Your body needs rest,' said Moss. 'Combined with the merry-go-down, you are fatigued and will shortly be asleep. After you have slept you will be refreshed and ready to continue.'

'No,' said Roger, chuckling. 'I don't mean explain why I'm getting sleepy, you dafty. I meant about Leatherfred what's-his-name.'

Moss smiled. 'My joke, Roger. I know your meaning.' His smile slowly faded as he continued. 'Leatherhead Barnstorm is a waghalter, a whiteliver, a windsucker. He is a malignant dwarf who has gone to the bad, consumed by evil.' He smiled again. 'He is the one you stabbed in the leg and then threw from the wall of stone before he could split my head asunder.'

'Oh, *that's* who that was.' Roger yawned again before continuing. 'He had awfully red eyes. Why's he doing this? What's he trying to do?'

'Because my Queen and I support the humans, he wishes to destroy them. He knows that with the Doomstone Sword and the destruction of the human race, he will become ruler of the dwarves. He will kill me and claim Queen Gwri's hand in marriage. To this end, he has created gorefiend followers and during the years of searching for the sword, he has murdered many of the Watchers. We must put an end to him.'

'But why is he so bad?' Roger flapped a hand over his mouth as he yawned. 'What made him like that?' He sank down on to one elbow and tried to focus on the dwarf.

54

Moss sat silently for a few moments before answering. 'There was a *thing* in the past, between the two of us. A trivial thing. But it has festered and grown like a merry-gall on a buttockrump. His greatest wish is for me to die by his hand. He has sworn an oath on the Twisted Toenail of the Wicked Princess – and an oath is a considerable undertaking for a dwarf. It must be fulfilled. The moon has taken his mind. He has nothing there but hatred for me. He must be stopped.'

'Right,' said Roger, his head lolling to the side. 'That's quite a lot of things we've to do. Not today, though. We'll stop him tomorrow. I'm going to have a little sleepy now. See you in the morning, Mossy.' He stretched out and laid his head on the inside of his upper left arm.

'Sleep well, Roger,' said Moss, covering him with the tartan blanket and then pulling the roof branches over the rest of the barricade. 'I'll guard your dream time.'

'Mossy?' mumbled Roger, stifling another yawn.

'Yes.'

'You . . . you really meant *mushroom* pie? Didn't you?'

'No, earthworms and mushrooms and herbs in pastry pie. Mushworm.'

'Oh . . .' said Roger, but before he could think about this, he drifted off.

CHAPTER
Ten

Roger awoke. He could hear birds tweeting and someone humming softly. He yawned, stretched, sat up and pushed back the tartan blanket. There was a clear blue sky above him.

'Rise, idle Roger,' said a voice as the humming stopped.

Roger looked around. The memories of yesterday came flooding back. He was still in the middle of a forest inside a small barricade. Mossbelly MacFearsome was breaking up the roof cover and scattering the wood.

'I go and empty body,' said the dwarf, throwing the last bit of wood away. 'Wait here until I return. Do not leave. This is for you – protection.' Moss unsheathed his dagger and dropped it inside the barricade.

Roger picked up the dagger and looked at it. It was small and felt extremely light in his hand. He sliced it through the air a couple of times and then chopped at a small branch in the barricade. The dagger cut the branch in two. Roger sat down and stared at the dagger in his hand. His head felt a little fuzzy and he was thirsty.

'You go now, empty body,' said Moss's voice.

Roger turned round and looked into the leathery face of Mossbelly MacFearsome peering over the barricade. Moss reached out and took the dagger from Roger.

'I'm thirsty,' said Roger.

'Good,' said Moss, pointing. 'Go that way, straight ahead, small water stream where you can drink.'

Roger looked at his watch; it was twenty minutes to six in the morning.

When Roger returned, the entire barricade had disappeared. Moss was sitting on the ground sharpening his weapons, the tartan blanket folded across his shoulders. The dwarf finished what he was doing, stood up and replaced his weapons around his body.

'How's your leg?' asked Roger.

'Better, thank you. Not as good as the other one but it is improving. Now, we go. Are you ready?'

'I think so,' said Roger. But Moss was already disappearing into the trees.

They walked for several minutes until they reached

57

a grassy bank leading down to a dual carriageway. On the other side of the carriageway was a field. Roger and Moss stood behind a tree watching the occasional car passing.

When the road was clear, they hurried across it and climbed up a small bank to a wire fence. Some cows in the field began moving towards them. Moss let out a deep roar and the cows turned and fled.

'This way,' said Moss, pulling up the wire and ducking into the field.

'You didn't need to do that,' said Roger, following.

'Keep up,' said Moss, without stopping or looking back. 'And do not be placing feet in cowsplats.'

Roger shook his head and followed the dwarf.

The sun was climbing into the clear sky as Roger and Moss began their journey to find the Witchwatcher of Auchterbolton. They avoided the dual carriageway, walking instead through the fields running along the side of the road, keeping out of sight of the passing traffic and anyone who might be on the lookout for a dwarf and a boy.

'How are you feeling this day?' asked Moss, as he

climbed over a crumbling dry-stone wall into another field. 'You slept like an ogre in the earth.'

'I'm fine,' said Roger. 'My head feels a little bit funny, but I'm OK.' Roger ran a few steps to catch up with the dwarf. 'Last night you said that this Leatherhead Barnstorm had the Doomstone Sword. How do you know?'

'We know. We can *feel* the Doomstone Sword. Its power works on all dwarves. Already my people are preparing for war against humans. If the sword is used to awaken the ogres . . .' Moss shook his head angrily. 'The sword is here and you must break it to stop its influence. *I* cannot destroy it. The magic contained in the sword is powerful. No dwarf can resist it! No dwarf can destroy it! I have told you this already! Do you have a daggle-tail's drawers stuffed in your ears? Do you not understand what I say?'

Roger did not reply. He walked in silence. He also noticed that Moss was beginning to limp again.

'You said last night that the main reason Leatherhead Barnstorm turned bad was because of something that happened with you,' said Roger, slowing his pace to match Moss. 'And why are his eyes so red? Why *does* he hate you so much?'

'Jealousy,' said Moss. 'Began one hundred and forty-three years ago, when we were both younghede dwarves.

I bettered him in the Great Frog Gobbing Contest. He never got above it. I was crowned champion and he was mocked as a fopdoodle. Red eyes are a sign of a malignant dwarf. One who has turned to the bad.'

'One hundred and—' Roger closed his mouth and walked along in silence, thinking about two young dwarves falling out *one hundred and forty-three years ago.*

'What is Frog . . . Gobbing?' he asked after a while.

Moss stopped walking and looked at Roger. 'Frog Gobbing is one of our greatest sports.' He puffed out his cheeks and made a spitting sound. 'Like that. The competition is held every four years. The Amphibian Games.'

Roger laughed. 'Like the Olympic Games?'

'Exactly,' said Moss. 'But completely different. Ours is open to all dwarves from anywhere in the Innerland. No ugly humans.'

'What happens?' asked Roger. 'How do you win?'

'What do you think happens?' Moss raised his arms, held his hands palms upwards and looked at Roger in disbelief. 'I've just told you! You put a frog in your mouth, and then . . . gob it as far as you can.'

'A live frog?' Roger screwed up his face.

'Of course it is alive,' Moss snorted. 'Only a fopdoodle would put a dead frog in their mouth.'

'Is that not a bit . . .' Roger hesitated, 'cruel?'

'Cruel?' Moss looked astonished. 'No, no, no. We love it. The skin of a frog tastes as sweet as tipsycake. The slimy secretions are delicious.'

'No, I meant . . .' said Roger, trying not to imagine the frogs splattering on the ground. 'What happened in the competition?'

'The contest lasted until only two were left for the final gobbing.'

'You and Leatherhead?' asked Roger, nodding. 'What then?'

'I wished him good gobbing and gave him a pat on the back for fortune.' Moss dropped his eyes to the ground. 'But he could not continue, so my mighty gob was declared a worthy winner. He has hated me since that time.'

'Why couldn't he continue?' asked Roger, trying to look Moss in the face.

Moss mumbled something, then cackled and turned it into a cough.

'Sorry,' said Roger. 'I couldn't hear what you said.'

Moss spoke up. 'He swallowed his frog!'

'What?' Roger stopped walking.

'He was about to gob . . . when I patted his back,' shouted Moss.

'Must have been some pat,' said Roger quietly.

'He claimed it was a blow. But it was just a comradely, good-natured, light tap – to wish him well.'

Roger bit his lip. 'That's why he hates you?'

'Yes,' said Moss. 'We have always been rivals. Various things have festered in his mind. I beat him easily in all competitive actions: tug o' war, mouse juggling, bushy beard tugging.' He shrugged and gave a little chuckle. 'Perhaps the frog still lives in his belly. I called him by the extremely amusing nickname of Natterjack for a long period of time.'

Roger looked blank. 'What does that mean?'

'Pah!' Moss waved a hand at Roger. 'Natterjack! He was using a toad that day when he gulped it down. Showing off. Everyone knows that a slimy frog gobs further than a dry warty toad.' He chuckled again. 'Natterjack! My humorous bantering is loved by all.'

'Are you sure?' said Roger, before he could stop himself.

'What?' growled Moss. 'Sure about what?'

'Um, nothing, it's just an expression,' said Roger quickly. 'You know, like, sure, amazing. Sure thing! Go on.'

'After King Golmar died,' said Moss, nodding his beard, 'Gwri became Queen. She had the choice between us for consort when she finished her father-mourning years, and she chose me for marriage. My wooing of her had been intense and she quickly realised I was vastly superior to that hoddypeak, Leatherhead.' He sighed deeply. 'We became betrothed after our first lip clap. And for our thirty years of betrothal Leatherhead has had a burrowing bug of jealousy eating his brain and poisoning his thinking thoughts. He is now completely mad.'

'Why did she choose . . . you?' Roger asked, desperately trying to keep his face straight.

Moss turned to look closely at Roger. 'You serious with that question?'

'I, um, just wondered.' Roger shrugged and smiled.

Moss drew himself up to his full height and glowered at Roger. 'I am a very handsome looker. My singing voice is better than most. My spitting distance is famed throughout the underground. All seek my cake-baking secrets. I am the finest warrior in the kingdom and the best poet for over two centuries. I am leader of the tug-o'-war team and I am Captain of the Royal Guard. I have more.'

'No, no,' said Roger, thinking how to change the subject. 'That's fine. I thought that it must be something like that. But why have you been engaged for *thirty years*?'

'It has always been thirty years,' said Moss. 'You cannot run into marriage quickly. There are too many roots and stones waiting to trip you. You must find out if you are truly compatible.'

'It's an awfully long time,' said Roger.

Moss stared hard at Roger before answering. 'No.' He shook his head, and then grunted. 'The seating arrangements usually take about ten years to plan.'

'What?' Roger looked disbelieving. 'Why?'

'Well,' said Moss, gesturing with both hands, 'obviously you must ensure that outbreaks of fighting are kept to a minimum. It's a nuisance if brawling breaks out during the wedding service.' He thought for a moment, before adding: 'Of course, once the speech-making has begun, that's a different matter. You are usually ready for some conflict.'

'That's completely—' Roger stopped talking, and put a hand over his mouth.

'What?' growled Moss, holding back. 'Completely what?'

'Fine,' said Roger. 'Completely fine.' He gulped. 'Sorry about that, swallowed a fly.'

Moss grunted again, then started to walk.

'What are those gorefiend things that attacked you?' asked Roger, following closely.

Moss did not answer but limped on until he reached a stone wall separating two fields. He stopped and muttered something as he began to climb over the wall.

'Sorry,' said Roger, reaching out a hand to help the dwarf. 'I didn't catch what you said.'

Moss clambered down into the other field and turned to look at Roger as he jumped down beside him. *'Grave wax,'* he thundered, looking furious.

'What?' said Roger, flinching and taking a step back.

'Grave wax, from humans buried in ground. It's what drips out of their coffin boxes. Leatherhead Barnstorm makes gorefiends out of the dead, to serve him. That's what we are up against, boy. Living dead things.'

Suddenly Roger felt cold.

CHAPTER
Eleven

'Sorry, boy,' said Moss, after a few moments' silence. 'Should not break my temper at you. You're not to blame for wanting to understand. But they are evil things. I do not like them.' He looked up at Roger. 'They are made from grave wax, and their spears are tipped with nails from their coffin-box lids. I really do not like them.'

'It's all right, Moss,' said Roger and, before he could stop himself, he patted the little man on his head and ruffled his beard. 'I understand. You can't help being a grumpy old dwarf.'

Moss made a choking noise; his eyes bulged, his face grew red and his hands hovered dangerously close to his weapons. He spluttered for a while and then, eventually, began to laugh.

'You're a good companion,' chortled Moss, slapping Roger on the back and knocking him forward several paces. 'For such a chitty-faced specimen of the ugly race. Come, let's save you from destruction.'

Roger and Moss continued their journey in the sunshine. Their progress was slow as they tramped through fields and negotiated fences and hedges; for a time they lay hidden as a tractor ploughed a furrow near them. Moss cursed and shook his fists as the machine drove off.

'Why are you on your own?' asked Roger, trying to keep the little man calm as they started walking again. 'Why aren't there more of you?'

'I've told you,' said Moss. 'Pay more attention to what I say. Dwarves cannot resist the Doomstone Sword spell.'

'But you're here,' said Roger. 'Even if you can't go against the sword, you're still here, on your own.'

Moss puffed out his chest. 'Because of who I am, I have been in training to fight against the power of the Doomstone Sword.'

'How?' asked Roger.

'By holding my breath until some of my warts burst and I fall down unconscious,' said Moss proudly.

Roger scratched at the top of his head. 'Does it work?'

Moss shrugged his shoulders and grunted. 'I am unsure. It certainly helps to combat a snottering buttocks spell, so it could be of benefit.' He nodded and continued. 'I should not be here. We are not meant to walk the Outerland. That's why we have Watchers – they communicate and pass on to us news about the progress of humanity.' He patted his satchel. 'And we only have one invisibility cloak left and it often has a mishap. It would take years to collect enough spiderwebs to make another.' Moss puffed out his chest. 'Anywise, I am the greatest warrior, and I know more about human ways than anyone else in the Innerland. I have familiarised myself with all of your habits and patterns of speech-talking.'

Roger smiled and looked up at the blue sky. He was thinking that if Moss was the best at *patterns of speech-talking*, the others must be pretty awful.

By late morning they found themselves standing on a slip road beside a sign pointing to Auchterbolton.

'What now?' asked Roger, looking down the road.

'Lady Goodroom dwells in Auchterbolton Castle,' said Moss, flexing his wounded leg on the hard surface. 'Location should not be difficult.'

'Is that it?' asked Roger, pointing. 'There.'

In the distance, sticking above some trees, was the top of a small turret. The sound of bagpipes drifted faintly in the air.

'I cannot see it,' said Moss, trying to stand on tiptoes and failing. 'But I hear the blow-bag noise. We go there.'

Roger and Moss walked towards the sound of bagpipes until they reached two iron gates lying open against a crumbling wall.

Beside the gates was a hand-painted notice on a pole:

Auchterbolton Highland Games
– this Saturday
Adults £5.00 – Small People and Mature
Individuals £1.50

'What are . . . mature individuals?' asked Moss, glowering at the noticeboard.

'Pensioners,' said Roger. 'Old age pensioners. You know, people who are very, very old – about forty.'

'That's not old,' said Moss. 'That's hardly any years.'

'Well, it is to us.' Roger fumbled through his pockets. 'Have you got any money on you?'

Moss continued to stare at the board while rubbing his hands over his weapons. 'Small people,' he said at last.

'You dislike small and old people? Why not let them pay same?'

'It doesn't mean what you think,' said Roger, still rummaging in his pockets.

Muttering to himself, Moss turned to Roger. 'I do not use money – I pay in gold.'

'You can't,' said Roger, grinning. 'And we don't want to attract attention. I've got three pounds and seven pence.'

'Means nothing to me,' said Moss. 'Why is your face smiling?'

'Because I've got an idea,' said Roger. 'Give me that blanket and take off your satchel.'

Moss took the tartan blanket from around his neck and passed it to Roger.

Roger opened the blanket and flapped it a couple of times. Then, holding it straight out in both hands, he looked at the dwarf. 'You're going to the Highland Games with your grandson.'

'What did you say?' Moss growled.

'This is how we are going to get in. Come here.'

Grumbling and muttering, Moss walked forward.

'Lift up your arms,' said Roger. He wound the blanket around Moss's body and tucked it under his armpits. 'There,' he said, trying not to laugh. 'You really look good in a kilt. Now for your trousers.'

He knelt and pulled up the trousers on Moss's uninjured leg. He stared at the knobbly limb sticking out of the boot. The leg had what looked like patches of thick fur sprouting randomly over its surface. The few bare areas were dotted with warts.

'On second thoughts,' said Roger, pulling the trouser leg back down, 'we'd be better off leaving your legs covered.'

'Why?' asked Moss. 'I have very fine leg limbs.'

'Um, yes,' said Roger, standing again. 'So you have . . . but . . . your wound. People might see your wounded leg and become curious. So best leave them both covered. Have you got a hat?'

Moss thought for a moment, nodded, bent down and opened his satchel. He pulled out a red bobble hat.

Roger made a face. 'Is that all you've got?'

'What's wrong with the hat?' Moss asked.

'Nothing, nothing,' said Roger quickly. 'It's a fine hat. Put it on and pull it down as far as you can. Tuck your hair in. And don't you say a word to anyone. Let me do all the talking.'

'Very well,' said Moss, glowering as he pulled the hat over his head, almost covering his eyes. 'I'll not speak.' He picked up the satchel and slung it over his shoulder.

Roger and Moss walked into the castle grounds. Tucked in on the left, just beyond the gates, was a table.

Standing beside it was an extremely large man. He had a round head with thinning hair, no neck, massive shoulders and a huge chest and stomach. Roger slowed down as he approached the intimidating figure. He had almost stopped walking when Moss gripped his arm and propelled him forward.

'Good morning,' said the large man in an extremely polite voice. He bowed slightly. 'How are you gentlemen this fine day?'

Roger and Moss stood in front of the table looking up at the man. He was immaculately dressed in a white shirt, dark tie and dark suit. His shoes gleamed.

'Hello,' said Roger, nervously placing three pounds on the table. 'Me and my grand . . . my grandfather have come for the Games. He's from the, um, Highlands.'

The large man beamed. 'Then there is no admission fee, young sir. Any visitors from the Highlands, or grandfathers and their grandsons, are allowed in for absolutely no charge. Please, take your money back.'

Roger quickly picked up his money. He could hardly believe his luck. They were getting away with it. 'Thank you. Thank you very much. Um, you wouldn't happen to know where we could find Lady Goodroom, would you?'

'I certainly would, young man. I have the pleasure to be her ladyship's butler. My name is Tobias Undercut.

Her ladyship is currently up near the castle. I'll phone ahead and announce your imminent arrival. You may even be expected.' He pulled a mobile phone out of his pocket. 'Your name, sir?'

'Eh, Roger. Roger Paxton, and . . . Moss Paxton, Captain Moss Paxton.'

'Thank you, Master Paxton. It is a pleasure to welcome you to Auchterbolton Castle, and of course your grandfather, the captain. It's always nice to meet someone from the Services. Straight up the driveway, right to the top, you can't miss it.'

'How will I recognise her ladyship?' asked Roger.

'Don't worry, young man,' said the butler. 'I think that she will recognise you. Your *grandfather* is not difficult to notice.' He pointed at Moss.

Roger turned to look at Moss. He saw a ridiculous-looking leather-faced dwarf in a red bobble hat, wrapped in a tartan blanket up to his armpits, gazing back at him.

'Right,' said Roger, nodding. 'Right. Um . . . I suppose he doesn't look terribly like my . . .'

'Not really,' said Tobias Undercut, pursing his lips and giving the slightest headshake. 'But off you toddle, I'll let her ladyship know you are coming. I think that she'll be delighted to meet your grandfather.'

Roger and Moss left the polite butler and continued

along the driveway until they reached an open area where large men in kilts were tossing huge tree trunks in the air. They passed a platform where girls and boys, also in kilts, were dancing with their hands held above their heads while pipers, standing on either side of the platform, puffed their faces out like balloons as their fingers darted up and down chanters and their elbows squeezed bagpipes.

Moss stuck fingers in his ears as he walked past the bagpipe players, and muttered to himself.

Roger pulled at the dwarf's arm. 'Don't do that,' he said, looking around. 'You'll draw attention to us. Why're you doing that?'

'Their playing is a maw-wallop,' said Moss, taking his fingers away. 'They are faffling and kee-kawing when they should be hudder-muddering. They're screeching like a bare-bottomed babe sitting on a hedgehog. I could play them out of vision.'

Roger just looked at Moss. He couldn't think of anything to say.

They walked past stalls selling things, and stalls where people were trying to win things. Horses with riders were jumping over fences, and cattle were being paraded in front of judges. A row of gleaming tractors was almost too much for Moss. He was feeling for his club, muttering and cursing, as Roger dragged him away.

'Earth diggers!' Moss shouted over his shoulder. Roger did his best to smother the outburst by laughing loudly and throwing his arms round the dwarf's shoulders. Several people turned to look.

'Ahaha-ahaha-ahaha,' Roger laughed, trying to sound convincing but failing miserably. 'That's a good one, a really good joke.'

Roger and Moss continued past vans selling candyfloss, ice cream and hot dogs. They reached a crowded beer tent.

'Would you look at that,' said a loud voice. 'Someone's let a wee tartan gorilla outa the zoo.'

Roger and Moss turned. A stocky man was standing at the entrance to the beer tent. He was waving a tumbler of beer in one hand and had a cigarette in the other. He turned to some men standing nearby and laughed.

'What's your tartan, wee man?' asked the man, looking back at Moss. He took a large swig of beer. 'Is it the *MacMonkey*?'

Moss started walking towards the man.

'Moss . . .' Roger tried to catch his arm. 'Don't, he's just—'

'Do not be worrying,' said Moss, shrugging off Roger. 'I'll not kill him, just give him some knowledge.'

'It's a talking monkey,' screeched the man, bending

down into Moss's face. 'Here, wee MacMonkey man, would you like a drink of—?'

Moss hit the man with an uppercut to the chin. The man's head jolted upright and he staggered backwards into the tent. There was the sound of breaking glass and then raised voices followed by loud thumps. Moss growled at the other men.

Two more men rolled out of the tent. They were holding each other by their shirts and were banging their heads together; they both let go at the same time and lay on the ground groaning. The noise in the tent grew louder as the fighting spread.

'What had that to do with knowledge?' Roger shouted, taking Moss by the arm and pulling him away.

'He'll know not to be rude,' said Moss, a touch smugly. 'A good lesson, knowledge never to be forgotten for an addlepated nincompoop.'

'Come on,' said Roger, pulling harder. 'I thought that you were all for peace and living together? I thought humans were the bad ones?'

'They are! We only fight if a provocation is thrust upon us.'

'You could've ignored him! We are not meant to be noticed! We are trying to blend in, not stick out like . . . like . . .'

'I am the Queen's champion!' Moss stuck his chest out. 'No one thrusts a provocation on me!'

'You're just bad-tempered.' Roger shook his head. 'Let's try and get to the castle without starting any more trouble.'

A policeman came running past, heading for the beer tent. Roger and Moss held their hands up to their faces and looked down at the ground.

As they neared the castle Roger could see a crowd of people gathered around two groups of men who were standing holding a thick rope. A tall man with spiky hair was holding a megaphone and bellowing at a crowd of spectators. Next to him was a girl with short dark hair, who was about Roger's age.

'Come on, then,' shouted the tall man in an English accent. 'There must be one of you who will help the teachers, just one more person is needed; the sides must be even before we can start. The farmers have eight men. One more for the teachers!'

Moss grunted happily, handed his satchel to Roger and began pushing his way through the spectators.

'Don't,' yelled Roger.

'Here we go,' said the man with the megaphone. 'We have a volunteer. We have a . . . small gentleman wearing a tartan something or other. And there appears to be an incident taking place over at the beer tent.'

77

Roger ran forward, but it was too late: Moss had already lifted the end of the rope and wound it over his shoulder and around his waist. Some of the spectators started laughing. On one side were eight hefty men all grinning and chatting happily. On the other side were seven rather weedy, grim-faced men and a tartan-wrapped dwarf. In the middle was a huge pile of steaming, slimy, brownish, yellowish goo.

'Take the strain,' yelled the man with the megaphone.

The rope was pulled tight. The teachers staggered forward.

'Steady. Steady. Back a little, farmers. That's it, now on the count of three. One . . . two . . . *three!*'

Both sides dug their heels in, and pulled. The farmers, laughing and chatting, began to walk backwards. The teachers slid towards the goo.

The girl with the short dark hair ran to the teachers and tried to encourage them.

'Pull, Moss,' yelled Roger. 'Pull, Moss!'

The people next to Roger started cheering, and then began to chant: 'Pull, Moss. Pull, Moss. Pull-moss. Pull-moss.' The entire crowd joined in. 'Pull-moss. Pull-moss.'

The teacher at the front was almost in the goo when Moss turned slightly to his left and began to pull. The slide of the teachers stopped. Moss grunted and jerked on the rope. The farmers slipped forward. Moss grunted again and the farmers inched further forward. They had stopped laughing.

The dark-haired girl jumped up and down and waved her hands in the air.

'We've got them, men!' shouted the teacher at the front. 'Keep pulling!'

The farmers lost the ground they had gained. Moss heaved harder. The crowd had stopped chanting and were cheering and clapping as they watched the farmers move nearer to the middle. Then suddenly it was all over. The farmers collapsed on the grass and were pulled through the gunge. The crowd roared. The teachers threw down their rope and hugged each other. Moss bowed, rubbed his wounded leg and walked off to great applause.

Roger saw the dark-haired girl turn to the man with the megaphone. She was pointing at Moss.

'I've told you, we are not meant to be noticed,' hissed Roger as he pulled the dwarf away from the crowd. 'Stop drawing attention to us! What was that all about?'

'I likes a good tug o' war,' said the dwarf happily. 'Could not withstand joining. And you heard the man with the voice. They're farmers.' Moss spat on the ground.

'You're disgusting,' said Roger as he hurried Moss along to the castle ahead of them.

'Here, gies us a shot,' said a familiar voice. 'Here's your money, mister. Now watch this, weans. Yer dad's gonny ring the bell for you and win a prize.'

Roger and Moss turned to see Wullie from their van journey beside a small woman and two little girls. They were in front of a Strong Man game tower. Wullie was holding a large mallet in his hands.

'Here we go, weans,' said Wullie, and with great difficulty he swung the mallet over his head. The mallet came down on the rounded button at the bottom of the tower. An arrow crept up and stopped at the halfway point. Beside the arrow was a message:

EAT A LOT MORE PORRIDGE – YOU ARE A WEAKLING!!!

'That's no right,' said Wullie. 'I was off balance. Give us another quid, pet, till I win the weans a prize.'

'No, Wullie,' said the small woman. 'You're no getting any more money to waste. You've spent enough on rubbish already. We've hardly got enough left for ice-cream poky-hats.'

'Give the man a bartering quid chip, Roger,' said Moss, as he walked over to Wullie and his family.

Roger sighed, took a pound coin out of his pocket and gave it to the fairground man standing beside the tower.

'See this, Wullie,' said Moss, taking the mallet in one hand. He swung it around and over his shoulder. The mallet blurred through the air and smacked down on the button. The arrow flashed to the top of the tower and clanged into the bell. The tower swayed and some flakes of paint floated down.

Moss turned to the man at the tower and held out his hand. 'Weans' prize.'

The man closed his mouth and started fumbling in a box. He pulled out a small plaster gnome wearing a red bobble hat and handed it to Moss. Moss took the gnome, his face turning red, and shoved it at Mrs Wullie. 'For weans, Wullie-wife, but do not keep, this is a *bad* mockery.' He bent down and scooped up several small stones at the base of the tower and held them out to Wullie. 'For the carriage driving,' said Moss, dropping the stones into Wullie's hand.

'*There* you are,' shouted a voice. 'At last. Come away, come away. We're in the library.'

Roger turned to see a large lady in a heavy tweed skirt and a green waterproof jacket. Standing beside her was the dark-haired girl.

'Are you—' began Roger.

'Of course I am. Come on, I've been looking for you. Maddie told me you were here.' She waved a hand, turned and walked towards the castle steps.

The dark-haired girl glared at Roger, then held up her fists. She kicked her right leg in the air three times, and then spun round and ran off in the opposite direction.

Roger and Moss watched the girl disappear into the crowd before following the lady up the stairs and into the castle.

As the castle doors closed, Wullie's wife looked at Wullie. 'Is that *gold*?'

'Aye, it is. It's gold right enough,' said Wullie, clenching his fist tight around the precious metal.

'How come that funny wee man gave you gold, Wullie?'

'Eh, I'm no that sure, pet. I think maybe ah did him a favour . . . once!'

'It must have been *some* favour. Come on, let's get out of here before he wants it back.'

Wullie and his wife scooped up their daughters and hurried away.

CHAPTER
Twelve

Roger and Moss were ushered into a large, book-lined room with glass-panelled doors looking out on to a patio.

'Do take a seat,' said the tweed-skirted lady, pointing at two armchairs. She smiled at Roger, a friendly smile in a very plump face. 'I'm Gwendolena Goodroom. Call me Gwen.'

Roger watched, fascinated, as Lady Goodroom's chins wobbled below her small, mobile mouth. She folded her arms over a considerable frontage and looked at Moss.

'And we've met before, Mossbelly MacFearsome. Captain Mossbelly MacFearsome, the great dwarf champion, betrothed to Queen Gwri.'

Moss stood up, slapped his chest, and bowed slightly. 'I remember, Lady Goodroom. It is a pleasant experience to meet you again. But I'm on a quest of vital importance.'

'The Doomstone Sword?' asked Lady Goodroom. 'I've heard it has been found. Has it been brought to Scotland?'

'Yes,' said Moss. 'Its power is here. This is where the Awakening will begin.'

Lady Goodroom shook her head and tutted. 'And this young man?' She flicked her hand in Roger's direction.

'A boy, Roger,' said Moss. 'He is my chosen Destroyer, to do what I cannot.'

'Tut-tut,' said Lady Goodroom. 'No contact with any humans except Watchers. They're your rules. You pay for advice and secrecy. Choosing a boy – a schoolboy. Really! Could you not do better than that?'

'I could not in a thousand years,' said Moss. 'He is a warrior. He will fight against strong enemies when there is no chance of winning. With my own eyes, I saw him wound Leatherhead Barnstorm and then cast him over a wall of stone with his bare hands. I was wounded myself and so could not—'

'Wounded!' said Lady Goodroom, moving towards Moss. 'Who did it? Let me see.'

'It's nothing,' said Moss, but he sat down and raised his leg. 'One of Leatherhead Barnstorm's gorefiends attacked me from behind.'

Lady Goodroom knelt down and looked into Moss's eyes. 'Leatherhead Barnstorm, eh? So that's what it's all about – the Great Frog Gobbing Contest? The frog feud?'

Moss's face began to turn purple.

'Excuse me!' said Roger, jumping to his feet. 'Before you see to Moss, I'd just like to say something. I've been out all night with this grumpy dwarf and I'm in a lot of trouble because of him. My mum thinks I've run away. The police are after me. I'd like to go home, but I can't. And I wasn't "chosen". I was forced into this. And I'm *not* a warrior!'

Lady Goodroom turned and stared at Roger for a few moments. She pursed her small lips. 'My, my, you've got a right feisty one here and no mistake. Perhaps a good choice after all, Captain Moss. Well done.' She held out her hand to Roger. 'I'm sorry if it seemed I was ignoring you. We'll do something about your poor mother in just a minute. But first I must see to—'

The door opened and the tall man from the tug o' war came into the room. The dark-haired girl slipped in behind him. She was holding the megaphone.

'Everything all right, Aunt Gwen?' asked the girl.

'Yes,' said Lady Goodroom. 'Sit down, both of you. We're just having a little chat.'

'Hello, me dear,' said the man. 'Heard you had company. One of your wee friends, is it? Messages from below ground and all that stuff?' He tapped his lips with a finger. 'Nuff said, shan't breathe a word. I was hoping Tobias would be here. Need to speak to him. Have you seen him?'

'Your lordship,' murmured a voice from the doorway, as the butler glided into the room.

'Ah, Tobias, old bean,' said the thin man. 'Need your help to move some bits of wood. Some blighter in a van just sideswiped our fence at the main entrance. Didn't stop, just shot out of the gates.'

'It's already done, your lordship,' said Tobias. 'I also have the miscreant's name and registration number if you wish to submit a claim for damages? It's the man who delivers our paper towels every week for the public toilets.'

'Oh, you mean *Wullie*,' said the thin man. 'I like him, he's a good sort. Well, it's just a fence, we'll forget it.' He looked at Lady Goodroom. 'Funny sort of day, me dear – there's a riot in the beer tent and the farmers are fighting the schoolteachers.'

'Oh, the poor teachers,' said Lady Goodroom. 'Can't you stop it, Pen?'

'That's the funny thing,' said Lord Goodroom. 'The teachers are winning, dashed odd.'

'Ah well, as long as they're enjoying themselves,' said Lady Goodroom. 'Now, we have more important business. This –' she pointed at Moss – 'is Captain Mossbelly MacFearsome and his companion, Roger. They are here on a matter of the utmost importance. This is my husband, Penrose, and our ward, Maddie.'

Roger looked puzzled.

'We are Maddie's guardians, her legal guardians,' explained Lady Goodroom. 'And you've already met our butler, Tobias.'

There were murmurs and nodding heads all round. Lady Goodroom spoke again. 'Penrose knows most of what I do in my capacity as Witchwatcher for the dwarves, although I don't really involve him in anything much. You're a little bit eccentric, dear.' She spoke loudly. 'Aren't you?'

'Batty as a bag of budgies,' said Lord Goodroom, nodding happily.

'And Maddie is the future,' said Lady Goodroom, smiling at the girl. 'She is learning what it means to be a Witchwatcher.'

Maddie stood in front of Roger and Moss and stared at them. 'Just so you know, I can do karate,' she said, concentrating on Roger. 'I'm a yellow belt already.'

'Oh, that's good,' said Roger, smiling at the intense girl in front of him and desperately trying to think of something impressive to say. She had mesmerising hazel eyes.

'And Tobias only knows a little of what I do,' continued Lady Goodroom, looking at her butler. 'My connection with the dwarves. But I don't think you know a great deal about it, eh?'

'As you say, your ladyship,' said Tobias. 'I've picked up a little here and there, but not quite the whole picture. Not my business.'

'Good man,' said Lady Goodroom. 'Well, it's time to bring you up to scratch. It looks as though there is going to be trouble. We could be in for a fight.' She looked to Moss.

Moss nodded and stood up.

'There are gorefiends walking the Outerland,' said Moss, taking off his satchel and placing it on a table. He winked at Roger and tapped his nose twice before continuing. 'They are led by Leatherhead Barnstorm, and they are after *this*.' Moss took out the hammer with the gold band and put it on the table. 'This is the only thing that can stop the destruction of the human race.'

For the next few minutes Moss explained his mission, how he had been tasked to destroy the Doomstone Sword before the ogres were awakened, and how he had met Roger and then been attacked by gorefiends.

'But what makes you think they'll come here, old chap?' asked Lord Goodroom. 'D'ye think they followed you?'

'Gorefiends have my scent in the Outerland,' said Moss. 'Being made from dead bodies, all body odours are very special to them.' He pointed at Roger. 'A gorefiend escaped when I was attacked and they now have the boy's scent as well. They found my location before, and

Leatherhead knows there is a Watcher in this area. He has killed many Watchers since he fled our realm. He will have gorefiends scouting the area and he has sworn to kill me. He may bring the Doomstone Sword this time.'

'But there's another reason why you're both here, and at the same time.' Lady Goodroom spoke quietly. 'You haven't quite given us the whole story, have you, Captain Mossbelly MacFearsome?'

Everyone looked at Lady Goodroom.

'What?' Maddie glanced at Moss, and then back at Lady Goodroom. 'Why are they both here at the same time?'

'The Great Frog Gobbing Feud began at a village near here,' said Lady Goodroom slowly. 'And *you –*' she pointed at Moss – 'are here to draw him out. You are the *bait*. His hatred of you is so strong that he would rather come here to kill you than do the sensible thing – raise the ogres. Am I right?'

Moss grunted and cleared his throat. His face above his beard was bright red. 'You have the truth of it, Lady Goodroom.'

'I knew it,' said Lady Goodroom, just a touch smugly. 'Leatherhead is blinded by his hatred of you, isn't he?'

Moss looked around at each person in the room. 'My Queen has been planning all along to save your race from

89

destruction. We hatched our plot. We let it be known that I was in the Outerland, with the hammer. That I was near the site of his – *hruuumph* – humiliation at the village of Fowlis Wester.' Moss tapped himself on the chest. 'I *am* the worm on the line to catch the gandygut.'

'But that's daft,' said Roger. 'You're saying that you're here so that Leatherhead comes after you? He wants you dead more than anything else? Why doesn't he just get on with raising the ogres and take care of you later. He's got the Doomstone Sword.'

'No.' Moss shook his head and took a deep breath. 'I *am* his main purpose. He has this inexplicable hatred of me. Like I told you, when he fled our realm he swore a sacred oath on the Twisted Toenail of the Wicked Princess that, if I were ever to appear anywhere in the Outerland, he would seek me out and kill me. He *must* fulfil that oath before he can do aught else.'

Lord Goodroom pressed a finger against his head and looked thoughtful. 'Twisted Toenail . . .' He pointed his finger in the air. 'Ah, got it, that's a nice wee pub, in Perth. Been there a few times . . .'

Lady Goodroom shook her head and mouthed a silent *no*.

'When he comes for me,' continued Moss, 'Roger will have a chance to smite the Doomstone Sword! To do what I as a dwarf cannot. And when the sword is broken and its power drained . . .' There was a long pause. 'Then I will fight Leatherhead, to the death.'

Roger glanced at the hammer lying on the table. He didn't feel too good. It had been fun when he had been with Moss in the woods and Moss had been talking rubbish and laughing and drinking. But here, in this room, what he was being asked to do did not feel nearly so amusing.

'Maddie's parents were Witchwatchers,' said Lady Goodroom, looking grim. 'When she was little, they fought him, but Leatherhead Barnstorm slew them. Maddie was fortunate to survive that terrible day. He is a fierce warrior.'

Moss nodded. 'He *is* a fierce warrior. But *I* am Mossbelly MacFearsome.'

Roger glanced at the girl. Maddie was standing very still; her shoulders were pulled back and her head was held high.

'Oh dear,' said Lady Goodroom. 'I had hoped this day would never come.' She puffed out her cheeks. 'Well, dwarf gold has funded my projects for many years, and it's also kept this old place from going under. We'll fight with you, of course. After all, it is we who you are trying to save.'

'So,' said Lord Goodroom, rubbing his hands together. 'There could be a bit of a ding-dong, eh? You with us, Tobias, old chap? You used to be a wrestler.'

'Most certainly,' said the butler, bowing slightly. 'Nothing would give me greater pleasure.'

'Me too,' said Maddie. She placed the megaphone on the floor, made two fists and pumped her arms back and forward vigorously. 'I'll fight.'

'We'll talk about that later,' said Lady Goodroom gently.

'When will the blighters come?' asked Lord Goodroom. 'And how many?'

'I think there will be many, and that they will come at dawn tomorrow.' Moss gestured out of the window at the Games. 'There are too many humans here now. And gorefiends like to return to graveyards for the dark hours.'

'Well, June mornings are very light,' said Lady Goodroom, walking over to the table. 'So they could be here in the early hours tomorrow.' She thought for a moment. 'That still gives us plenty of time to prepare for an attack. In the meantime, this –' she lifted the gold-banded hammer and walked over to a large painting of a duck hanging on a wall – 'goes somewhere no one can get it.' The picture on the wall swung outwards revealing a small safe. Lady Goodroom fiddled with a combination lock, opened the safe, popped the small hammer inside and then turned the dial several times. 'There now, only Penrose and I know the combination.'

'And I can't remember it,' said Lord Goodroom, rolling his eyes.

'Now,' said Lady Goodroom, 'I'll attend to the captain's wound and then I'll phone Roger's mum to stop her worrying.'

'How will you do that?' asked Roger.

Lady Goodroom smiled. 'I'll put a spell on her, of course. After all, I *am* a witch.'

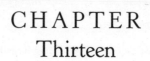

CHAPTER
Thirteen

Lord Goodroom, Maddie and Tobias left the room as Lady Goodroom set to work on Moss's leg. She stripped the bandage and then bathed the wound. 'You'll be fine,' she said, wrapping a fresh bandage around his leg. 'It's doing nicely and I've put a healing spell on it to speed the process.'

She turned to Roger as Moss hobbled out.

'Now, what's your mother's first name?'

'Er, June,' said Roger. 'What are you going to do?'

'Just a little magic to take away her worry,' said Lady Goodroom, sitting down. She indicated the seat beside her and passed a telephone to Roger. 'Just dial your number, blow gently into the phone three times and then give the phone back to me. Don't say anything until I have woven the spell.'

Roger dialled his home number. His mother answered the phone after two rings. Roger blew three times.

'*Hello. Who's there? Is that you, Roger?*'

Lady Goodroom took the phone from Roger. 'June? I'm a friend of Roger. I have a message for you. Just listen. Just listen. Are you listening? Good. June, you are serene. June, you are tranquil. June, you are calm.' Lady Goodroom began to hum softly. She handed the phone back to Roger.

'Hi, Mum,' said Roger.

There was a few seconds of silence, then his mother's voice. 'Hello, Roger,' she said calmly. 'Are you all right?'

'Er, yes, Mum, I'm fine.'

'Good, Roger. When will you be coming home?'

'I'm not too sure. It won't be very long, a day or two. Are you all right?'

'Oh yes. I was quite worried. But now that I've heard from you, I'm fine. Are you getting enough to eat?'

'Yes, thank you.'

'Good. Make sure you clean your teeth. Come home soon, Roger, we're missing you. Bye then, love.'

'Bye, Mum.' Roger put the phone down.

'Good,' said Lady Goodroom. 'That takes care of that. Unfortunately my spells are not powerful. That one only lasts for a couple of days and then the poor woman will be twice as bad as she was. Now, food and drink for both of you, then you can relax. When our Highland Show finishes, we'll talk again.'

'Thank you for doing that,' said Roger. He hesitated. 'Can I ask you something?'

'Of course,' said Lady Goodroom. She laughed. 'You are part of this, and I've never had a fully-fledged Destroyer in my little castle before.'

Roger felt exasperated. 'I'm *not* a Destroyer!' He held up his hands. 'Honestly! I didn't mean to stab Leatherhead. And I didn't throw him over a wall. I was trying to catch him!' Roger raised his voice. '*He* just won't listen! *He* ignores what I say! *He* just goes on all the time about—'

Lady Goodroom waved a finger in front of Roger. 'Don't shout, Roger. You don't need to explain. I know you're not a warrior. I've been dealing with dwarves most of my life, so I understand how they think, how they behave – particularly male dwarves. However, my relationship with Queen Gwri is excellent. We have tea together at least once a month when I make my report.'

'That was my question,' said Roger quietly. 'What is it you report? Why do you report on . . . us?'

Lady Goodroom smiled. 'So that's what's bothering you. Well, don't worry. I report mainly on the environment and the progress of the human race. I support many good causes and contribute to them using dwarf gold. Unfortunately I can only use very small amounts of their gold so as not to affect the financial markets.' She gave a little nod. 'I also, occasionally, use what little talent I have with spells to help people reach the correct decisions regarding the environment. You know that plastic pollution has reached a disgraceful level? That it threatens our seas and our marine life? Well, I'm pushing hard for biodegradable solutions for other sorts of packaging. Persuading people is difficult, though.' She gave the slightest of winks. 'Even with a little magic. But,' she continued, 'most of my work is involved in protecting the standing stones in my area. I make sure they are not disturbed by any building or digging. That cannot be allowed to happen. I'm on the planning board, so I see all applications.' She dropped her voice a little. 'There is a network of us Witchwatchers and Warlockwatchers all over the country, doing the same sorts of things. We even have a get-together once a year in the dwarf queen's royal apartments.' She smiled. 'It's a beautiful place, the Innerland. You wouldn't think being underground could be so marvellous, but it is. The weather is always so pleasant.'

'But—' began Roger.

Lady Goodroom pursed her lips and made a gentle *shushing* sound. She looked around, then leaned closer and took Roger's hand. 'We are also planning the best way to make sure that in one hundred and thirty-seven years, or hopefully much sooner, dwarves, ogres, humans and the others can all live happily together again.'

'I thought,' said Roger, 'that the humans were all going to get killed if they hadn't sorted themselves out by then?'

'That *was* the old plan,' said Lady Goodroom. 'That's what was meant to happen. It was set up that way in the olden days, hundreds of years ago. But Queen Gwri is a very modern dwarf. She knows that what was proposed all those years ago should not apply now. The races must learn to live together; you cannot destroy one of them because you don't like the way they behave. There are other ways of sorting things. Queen Gwri knows this; she is an intelligent thinker with very good ideas. She wants the dwarves to use their many abilities to aid humans. Now! Stop them ruining the Earth. We are planning changes in dwarf law to bring about a reconciliation of the species. Our plans are well under way, but . . .' She leaned even closer and whispered, 'The main problem is with stubborn, bone-headed *male* dwarves who believe that a law passed is a law for ever. We might not sort it in my lifetime, but it will happen, I'm sure.'

'Does Moss know about this?' asked Roger.

'Oh yes, he knows,' said Lady Goodroom. 'Queen Gwri's got him convinced, and he's so in love that he would do anything for her. Anyway, female dwarves do most of the thinking. Male dwarves are not generally the greatest thinkers. Their minds tend to concentrate on the simpler things in life.'

'Yes,' said Roger, nodding his head. 'I know.'

'And it was all going so well,' sighed Lady Goodroom 'Until that mad wee . . . that *Leatherhead Barnstorm* went crazy some years ago and started searching for the Doomstone Sword. It was harmless under the water – it should have stayed there. And now he's got it.' She frowned at Roger. 'Rampaging around the country with his band of foul creatures . . .' Lady Goodroom shook her head. 'Horrible, horrible things. Murdering Witchwatchers. Maddie's parents were close friends of ours, you know.'

'Maddie must feel very angry and upset,' said Roger.

'Maddie's just fine,' said Lady Goodroom, letting go of Roger's hand and sitting back. 'She was very young when it happened . . . and she has no real memory of it. We've brought her up as our own. Our lovely girl.' She paused, then dabbed at her eyes with the back of her hand and gave a little laugh. 'She can be quite a handful, though.'

Roger nodded, and tried to give his version of an understanding smile.

Lady Goodroom sniffed loudly and dabbed her eyes again.

Fresh from a shower and with a borrowed change of clothes, including slightly worn trousers and a gaudy tartan jumper from the castle gift shop, one hour later Roger was sitting in the library with his eyes closed when there was a loud rap on the patio doors. His eyes shot open.

Maddie was standing outside, her face pressed against the glass, a hand shading her eyes.

Roger got up and went outside. But there was no sign of Maddie outdoors. He stood for a moment, then came back in, closing the doors. As he turned round, Maddie was standing right there.

'Aaargh!' Roger jumped back. 'How did you do that?'

'I'm fast,' said Maddie, staring intently at Roger. 'Went in a side door.' Her hazel eyes had flashes of green and yellow. 'Why are you the Destroyer? What makes you so special? Are you really a great warrior?' She took a step backwards and put her hands on her hips. 'You're only a boy, you're about the same age as me. Why you, eh?'

Before Roger could say anything, Maddie reached out and poked a finger into his chest.

'I'm not *allowed* to fight,' she said, still poking. '*I'm* too important for the future. *I've* to stay out of it. *I've* to hide in my room. What can *you* do that I can't?'

Roger took a deep breath.

'You can't even *speak*,' said Maddie, poking Roger's chest again. 'Moss says you fought Leatherhead Barnstorm, wounded him and then threw him over a wall?'

'Stop that!' Roger said, angrily pushing her finger away. 'No, I'm not special. I'm not a warrior. Everything was an accident. Moss only sees what he wants to see and ignores everything else. I didn't fight anyone. I don't want to fight anyone or anything. That crazy, grumpy dwarf got me into this, so leave me alone.'

'You sure?' asked Maddie, hands on hips again. 'You're just an ordinary boy? Not special?' She made a face. 'Can't fight?'

'No,' said Roger. 'Not special. Not anything.'

Maddie smiled. 'Good.' She held out her hand. 'We'll be friends, then. Shake.'

Roger reached out and took her hand. She had a lovely smile, all crinkly.

'Would you do me a favour, seeing as we're friends now?' asked Maddie, pumping Roger's hand.

Roger hesitated. 'If I can.'

'Tell Aunt Gwen that you think I would be an enormously great help when the gorefiends attack. Would you do that, please?'

'Well . . .' Roger looked away from the smile and sparkling eyes. He began to examine the furniture and walls. 'Why?'

'Because . . .' Maddie let go of Roger's hand and took a fighting stance. '*I'm* a warrior and *I* can fight.' She swung her arms about and kicked out with her right leg several times. 'As I said, I'm a yellow belt.'

'Um . . .' Roger moved back from the flying kicks. 'The gorefiends are really, really horrible things. They're dangerous.'

'So am I,' said Maddie, breathing deeply. 'But will you speak to her? Will you?'

'Well . . .' began Roger.

'Please,' said Maddie, then her smile faded and her eyes filled with tears. 'You know what he did to my parents . . . I know I was only small, but . . .' Maddie's voice grew husky. 'I've only got photographs to look at now . . . to remember Mum and Dad properly. I love Aunt Gwen and Uncle Pen *so* much, just like real parents, even though I know we're not actually related. But . . .' She gave a shivering sigh. 'I really would like to have the . . . the real ones still here. *Please*, Roger, say you'll speak to her.'

Roger swallowed hard and nodded his head. 'OK.'

'Good.' Maddie leaned forward and gave Roger a quick peck on the cheek. 'I knew we would be friends as soon as I saw you. Thank you.' She turned and walked out of the door.

Roger raised his hand and touched his cheek.

'Oh, I meant to ask you . . .' Maddie's head popped back round the door, she was smiling again. 'Do you like my hair this way?' She gave her head a little shake.

'Y-yeah,' Roger stammered. 'It-it's nice.'

'Good.' Maddie's smile grew wider. 'It's a bob cut.' She giggled a little. 'I think it suits me. Don't forget to speak to Aunt Gwen. And I do like your *new* jumper. You wearing it for a bet?'

The door closed. Roger stood for a few moments looking down at the jumper he had been given. He was still touching his cheek.

Around seven o'clock people started drifting away from the Highland Games, and by eight o'clock the last car and trailer pulled out of the estate, leaving it empty apart from the marquees and farming machinery. At nine o'clock Lord and Lady Goodroom, Maddie and Tobias Undercut joined Roger and Moss in the library.

'Now, then,' said Lady Goodroom, wedging herself into a chair. 'Captain Moss, you are positive that Leatherhead Barnstorm and his gorefiends will come here looking for you . . . and the hammer?'

'Yes.' Moss nodded. 'He will come for me. He cannot wait to slaughter me dead to the ground and keep his oath sworn on the Twisted Toenail of the Wicked Princess.'

'What *is* this twisted toenail thing?' asked Maddie. 'That's the second time—' She stopped as Lady Goodroom waved her hand dismissively.

'Not now, dear,' said Lady Goodroom. 'I'll tell you all about it later.' She gave a little shudder. 'It's a terrible story. Horrible.'

'So, who are these gorefiend chappies?' asked Lord Penrose, looking at Moss. 'What are we up against?'

'They are made from grave wax,' said Moss. 'Buried humans, their drippings. Barnstorm uses dark magic, turns them into fiends who obey him.'

'They are very polite,' said Roger. 'Even when they are killed.'

'They are always polite,' said Moss. 'They are *dead* polite. Because they do not fear death. They are already dead.'

'We'll make our stand here,' said Lady Goodroom. 'In this room. We'll move the furniture around to face the patio. Hopefully we can surprise them. Now, weapons. What have we got, Penrose?'

'Bring them in, Tobias, old bean,' said Penrose, nodding to the butler.

Tobias Undercut stood up, bowed slightly, and left the room. Seconds later he returned carrying a bulky grey blanket. He placed the bundle on a table and pulled back one corner to reveal an assortment of weapons: an old bolt-action rifle with a clip of bullets, a crossbow and two bolts, several golf clubs and a slightly broken croquet mallet.

'Mmm,' said Lady Goodroom, rubbing her chins. 'Is that all? I thought we had some shotguns?'

'Rusted or broken beyond repair, your ladyship.'

'Well, we'll just have to make the best of it, then,' said Lady Goodroom. 'Captain Moss, you won't need anything, as you've brought your own weapons. Penrose, you couldn't hit anything with a rifle and I hate the things. Tobias, can you shoot?'

'I can, your ladyship.'

'Good, you take the rifle. Penny, dear, you better have the five-iron, you're a fine golfer.'

Lord Goodroom beamed. 'Jolly good, old girl, my favourite club.'

'And I'll fire the crossbow,' said Lady Goodroom.

'That just leaves you, Roger.' She paused. 'Take the croquet mallet for self-defence, but you're not to be involved in any fighting. You'll be at the back of the room, hidden, ready to spring out as soon as you see the Doomstone Sword, then to smash it with the hammer. I'll go and get it for you now.'

'I suppose so,' said Roger. His mouth felt dry and he had an ache between his shoulder blades. Lady Goodroom started towards the picture of the duck.

'*Hmmmumph.*' Maddie elbowed Roger.

'Um,' began Roger. 'Do you think that Maddie might—?'

'No!' shouted Lady Goodroom, spinning round and holding up her hand. 'Maddie is not taking part in any of this. She is too young and has been through far too much. You –' she wagged a finger at Roger – 'are also too young, but you are named as the Destroyer so you must do exactly that. Destroy the sword, if you can. And if we are defeated, escape out of the door and get to Maddie's room. She'll show you where to hide. There are plenty of hiding places in this old heap. But they should leave you alone if they get the hammer and ki— capture us.'

'But Aunt Gwen, I can—' Maddie jumped to her feet.

'Maddie, enough!' Lady Goodroom shouted. 'Since your parents . . . Well, we've brought you up. We are your legal guardians. You're all we've got, and we're all you've got. And you'll do as you are told!' She went back to her seat. 'That's all there is to be said on the subject.'

Maddie stood for a moment, shoulders hunched, then she turned around and stormed out, slamming the door behind her.

Lady Goodroom sighed. 'She wants to avenge her parents. I understand that, but we can't let her, she's too precious. Too important for the future.'

'No, we can't,' said Lord Goodroom, shaking his spiky hair. 'But she's got a mind of her own, that one.' He tut-tutted, then chuckled. 'Don't know what we'll do when she's older. She'll be off exploring jungles or climbing cliffs as quick as winkie.'

'No she won't,' said Lady Goodroom softly. 'Being a Witchwatcher will give her all the adventures she'll need.'

Moss nodded his head in a knowing manner. 'Nurslings can be much trouble. My fledgling sister caused a mountain of shame. The trouble she inflicted on our family when she was immature . . .' He gazed into the distance.

There was a few moments' silence.

'What did she do?' prompted Lady Goodroom.

'Who?' Moss looked puzzled.

'Your sister, man,' said Lord Penrose.

'She cut off her beard.' Moss dropped his head and stared at the floor, muttering to himself.

Lady Goodroom's mouth trembled as she tried not to burst out laughing. 'Right,' she said, coughing a little. 'I'll put a trap-spell on the patio doors. It will only work once, but it'll give us a small advantage for a moment or two.' She walked over to the patio doors and flickered her hands around the door frames while muttering to herself. There was a very faint crackle and a couple of blue sparks flared briefly, and then vanished.

'There now, that's done,' said Lady Goodroom, walking back and picking up her crossbow. She turned to her butler. 'Tobias, make sure your rifle is in working order, the bolt looks a little rusty. It would be—'

'*What was that?*' Roger pointed towards the patio. 'I heard something!'

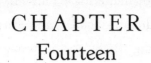

CHAPTER
Fourteen

Everyone turned and looked towards the patio doors.

The late evening sun was casting long, broken shadows across the library floor. There was a faint *skittering* noise.

'They're coming.' Lady Goodroom spoke softly without moving her lips. She bent down, braced the crossbow on the floor with her foot and pulled the bowstring back. She straightened up and loaded one of the bolts.

'Lady Goo—' Roger gulped hard.

'Not now, Roger,' hissed Lady Goodroom.

'Lady Good—' Roger tried again.

'*Shussh.*' Lady Goodroom glared at Roger.

Roger took a deep breath and shouted: 'Lady Goodroom – you didn't give me the hammer.'

'Oh—' Lady Goodroom looked across the room to the picture of the duck on the far wall.

'Stay!' shouted Moss as Lady Goodroom began to move. He looked at Roger. 'What foolishness are you spouting? If he has the Doomstone Sword, I'll give you *this*.' He slapped his beard and chest. 'Now arm yourself, boy, and be ready to act when I say so.'

Roger, puzzled, lowered his right hand and took hold of the croquet mallet. His knees began to shake. He tried to hold them steady but there was a definite tremor.

Moss stood perfectly still, his axe and sword held ready.

Lord Goodroom took up a golfing stance, his eyes fixed on the doors.

A small, bent-over shadow flitted briefly on the wall.

'Wait,' whispered Lady Goodroom.

Silently, the handle on the patio doors turned. The doors swung open and the setting sun filled the entire room with a golden glow. Roger's mouth was completely dry.

There was another *skittering* noise from outside. Roger lifted the mallet.

There was a brilliant flash. Two gorefiends were caught in the open doorway, sparks and smoke pouring out of them as they collapsed back on to the patio. Two more gorefiends jumped over them and entered the room.

'Now!' screamed Lady Goodroom, swinging the crossbow and firing. The bolt went through both gorefiends; yellow smoke and gunge spewed and bubbled as they fell. The doorway filled with gorefiends.

'Fore!' shouted Lord Goodroom. He swung his golf club as though playing a shot. The club head hit the leading creature under the chin. The other gorefiends stopped to watch as their companion flew over their heads out of the room.

'Jolly good shot.'

'Well played.'

'Handles that iron very well.'

Then they charged.

Lord Goodroom swung his golf club some more. Moss's axe and sword twirled and flashed. Lady Goodroom loaded and fired her remaining bolt, then used the crossbow as a club. The battle raged as the dead creatures poured into the room. Gorefiends were cut down, clubbed or splattered against the walls . . . but more kept coming.

A gorefiend ducked under Lady Goodroom's swinging crossbow and scrabbled across the floor. It stopped in front of Roger, who was frozen to the spot.

'Peek-a-boo,' said the gorefiend, grinning fiendishly. 'I see you. Not playing?'

The gorefiend lunged with its horrible spear. Roger twisted to the side. The gorefiend's spear went through the air and into the front of a chair. Roger, without thinking, raised the mallet and slammed it down on top of the creature's head.

'That was not very nice . . .' said the gorefiend, sinking to the floor.

'There's too many,' screamed Lady Goodroom, as she laid about her. 'Tobias, shoot!'

The butler appeared next to Roger and worked the bolt on his rifle. He aimed at the snarling gorefiends in front of him, and then at the last moment turned – and shot Lord Goodroom in the back.

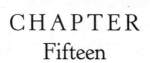

CHAPTER
Fifteen

The *crack* of the rifle made everyone stop fighting. Lord Goodroom gave a small shout, stumbled a few steps and fell face down on the floor.

'Penrose!' Lady Goodroom dropped her crossbow and knelt at her husband's side. 'Tobias! What have you done? You've shot Penrose by mistake!'

'No mistake,' said a voice from the patio.

A dwarf with a heavy cloak around his shoulders limped his way through the crowd of gorefiends. He had a battle-axe strapped to his back, and resting on his shoulder was a gleaming silver sword. Apart from his red eyes he looked remarkably like Moss. He stood over the body on the floor and stared at Lady Goodroom. 'I have learned that you have in your possession the only artefact that could foil my plans,' he said, then swung the Doomstone Sword from his shoulder and pointed it at Lord Goodroom's neck. 'Give me the hammer, if you want to save him. He might still be alive.'

'B-but . . .' stammered Lady Goodroom, looking at the dwarf. 'I don't understand. What—'

'The hammer!' yelled the dwarf, placing the tip of the sword against the back of Lord Goodroom's neck. 'Quick, or I'll separate his head from his body.'

Lady Goodroom got to her feet, tears running down her face. She looked at the butler and shook her head. 'Why?'

Tobias shrugged his massive shoulders. 'Why? Why *not*? My master made generous offers to several of us, to report on the Watchers. Money, power, I'm going to be very rich now I have delivered his sworn enemy into my master's hands.'

'You dumpling-headed human,' said Moss. 'You believed promises from Leatherhead Barnstorm?'

'I am a dwarf. I keep my promises,' thundered Leatherhead. 'He'll be well rewarded, as will the others who watch the Watchers.' He pointed at the butler. 'But *he* will be my second in command for delivering *you*.'

'You hear that, ladyship?' said Tobias, closing the patio doors and turning the key. '*I'll* have servants for a change.'

'Slaves, more like,' said Moss.

Tobias shrugged again. 'Whatever. Slaves will be acceptable.'

'*Enough*,' screamed Leatherhead, still pointing the

114

Doomstone Sword at the back of Penrose's neck. 'No more bluttering. Now, or he loses his head.'

'All right! All right!' Lady Goodroom moved through the gorefiends until she reached the picture of the duck.

'*Moss?*' hissed Roger, his eyes flitting from the gorefiends to Lady Goodroom.

There was no reply.

'Moss!' Roger looked at Moss.

The dwarf appeared to be holding his breath. His body was trembling and sweat was pouring down his face. As Roger watched, Moss tried to raise his sword. But his arm shook violently and his sword fell to the floor.

'Moss!' screamed Roger.

Moss blew out a huge puff of air. 'I . . . can do . . . nothing,' he gasped. His shoulders slumped and his arms flopped uselessly by his sides. 'The Doomstone Sword is too powerful.'

Lady Goodroom swung the picture away from the wall and put her hand on the dial.

Tobias stepped forward and pressed the muzzle of the rifle to her head. 'Be very careful or I'll put a bullet through your brain.'

Lady Goodroom looked contemptuously at the butler as she turned the dial. She opened the safe, reached in and pulled out the hammer with the gold band.

115

Tobias snatched it from her. 'Is it the one?' he asked, passing the hammer to Leatherhead.

'Yes,' said Leatherhead, with a great sigh. He looked at Moss. 'And now . . . for this poopnoddy, this trundletail, this mobard! I have waited a long time for this. My revenge shall be as sweet as tipsycake on the tongue.'

Moss stared back at Leatherhead. 'I am not afraid. Do your worst, you whiteliver. You are lunar mad, I can see it in your eyes.'

'Please, master,' said one of the gorefiends. 'May we kill them now in a slow and disgustingly painful way?'

Leatherhead nodded. 'Yes, we'll kill all of them. But MacFearsome must die slowly, and by my hand – in great agony.' He pointed the Doomstone Sword at Roger. 'For wounding me, the whifling dies first. Kill him now.'

The gorefiends lifted their spears and shuffled forward.

Roger looked at Moss. The dwarf was standing with his head lowered.

Roger bent down and snatched up a gorefiend's spear lying at his feet. *'Moss!'* he screamed. 'Help!'

Moss looked up. His face was twisted with pain. 'No!' His clenched fists shook. 'I cannot . . . fight . . . against the holder . . . of the . . .'

Roger crouched. He waved the spear from side to

side as the gorefiends closed in. But it trembled in his grasp.

Suddenly there was a loud roaring noise from outside. A large shadow hurtled across the patio and the doors exploded as a gigantic claw with curved talons smashed into the room. Glass and splinters of wood sprayed over the packed gorefiends. A huge red shape, roaring and belching smoke, followed the claw.

Roger, torn between relief and terror, tried to make sense of what he was seeing. The red shape was a tractor and the claw was a large scoop-bucket fixed on the front. Sitting in the driver's seat of the tractor was Maddie! She was steering one-handed and bellowing through a megaphone:

'All aboard the gorefiend express!

'Have your tickets ready!

'Next stop – Splatterville!'

The tractor tore around the library, chasing down gorefiends and crushing furniture. The bucket on the front of the tractor was scooping up squealing gorefiends and then thumping down, mashing them flat. Tobias Undercut threw himself to one side as the machine thundered towards him.

Leatherhead Barnstorm, screaming with rage, dodged around the careering tractor and, swinging the Doomstone Sword from side to side, cut his way through the scurrying gorefiends. He reached the broken doors, stumbled through the wreckage and ran across the patio. Tobias Undercut lumbered after him.

The tractor spun round in a tight circle, narrowly missing Lord Goodroom, and turned to head after the fleeing butler. Lady Goodroom, ignoring the carnage around her, went to her husband and knelt down at his side. The scoop-bucket on the tractor then clipped a bookcase and demolished an ornately decorated table. Maddie tried to follow the fleeing Leatherhead Barnstorm, but missed the wrecked doors and punched a hole through the side of the library wall instead. The tractor juddered to a halt, half in and half out of the room. The surviving gorefiends scrambled over the rubble and fled squealing out of the doors.

Maddie jumped from the driver's seat, threw down the megaphone, and ran to Lord Goodroom, shouting, 'Uncle Pen! Are you OK?'

Roger started after Maddie, then stopped dead as he heard an ominous creaking followed by a loud groaning. He glanced up to see that the wall above the tractor was cracking. The crack zigzagged up the wall and across the ceiling. There was a loud rumble as a large chunk caved in, flattening the last of the gorefiends and smothering the tractor. The ceiling began to bulge.

With the Doomstone Sword gone, Moss was finally released from its power. He shoved Roger out of the way just as the ceiling collapsed. Plaster poured down in a curtain of dust. A chunk of masonry hit Moss on the side of the head and he fell. He was immediately covered in the wreckage pouring down from the room above.

Roger tried to go to Moss, but a cast-iron bath bounced on the floor in front of him. He almost exploded with fright. A hand basin landed beside the bath and smashed in pieces across the floor. Water began to spray through the hole in the ceiling.

Roger could no longer see Mossbelly MacFearsome.

CHAPTER
Sixteen

Roger stood, shoulders hunched, hardly daring to move. He could see Lady Goodroom and Maddie were still kneeling beside the body of Lord Goodroom. They were untouched, apart from bits of plaster clinging to their hair and shoulders.

'Moss!' Roger pulled a set of bathroom scales from the top of the rubble and then tugged at a half-buried chair. It wouldn't budge. He dug his hands into the wreckage and tried to free the chair.

'Need help—' Roger looked around, coughing as the dust caught the back of his throat. He stood up and took a few stumbling steps towards the others. He put out a hand and touched Maddie on the shoulder. 'Is Lord Goodroom . . . all right?' he asked.

Maddie pushed him away, crying.

'Stop that, dear,' said Lady Goodroom, squeezing Maddie's arm. 'That's not doing any good. Help us, Roger.

Help us turn him over. Just a little! I need to see if the bullet went straight through.'

Roger bent down. Carefully and gently they moved Lord Goodroom on to his side.

Lord Goodroom's eyes fluttered open. He looked up at his wife. 'Hello, old gal. What happened? Feel as though a mule kicked me. Did we lose? You're looking a wee bit . . . dusty.'

'You were shot, dear,' said Lady Goodroom, wobbling furiously and dripping tears. 'Our butler shot you. The man you befriended and gave a job to shot you in the back!'

'By jingo,' said Lord Goodroom. 'The blackguard. Is it bad?'

'Don't know yet,' said Lady Goodroom, gently pulling at the clothing around the wound. 'I'll know in a moment.' She glanced at Roger. 'Is Moss all right?'

'I don't think so,' answered Roger, his voice choking. 'He got hit really hard by a big lump of stone. I think he's . . . gone!'

Just as Roger spoke, the pile of rubble moved. The chair was shoved away, then two hands emerged and started pushing the debris aside. A grey face and body appeared. It was Moss. He moaned and put his head in his hands.

'Moss! You're all right!' Roger stumbled over to the dwarf. 'Moss, are you . . . ? Can you . . . ?'

'I am a little turngiddy,' said Moss, taking his hands away and opening his eyes. 'I am trying to take control of my brain – it departed from my head for a period of time.'

'You were hit hard,' said Roger. 'You've got an awful lump. It looks terrible, like an egg.'

'Dwarves have thick bone heads,' said Moss, slowly getting to his feet with help from Roger. 'And I've got better bone thickness than most.' He took a few staggering steps towards Lady Goodroom. 'How's lordship?'

'The bullet went straight through his right side just above his hip,' said Lady Goodroom, without turning round. 'It's a flesh wound, and it's bleeding. I'm going to put a coagulating spell on it – I've got the right herbs and potions in the kitchen. We'll take him there.'

'Can I assist?' asked Moss, walking unsteadily over to where Lord Goodroom lay.

'Help me lift him, if you can,' said Lady Goodroom. 'Please.'

Moss bent down, slid his forearms under Lord Goodroom and lifted him off the floor. With Lady Goodroom and Maddie hovering close by, Moss carried the wounded man out of the room.

Roger stood alone. He looked around at the devastation,

sighed deeply and began to follow the others. He had only taken a few steps when a large piece of floorboard with a toilet pan and cistern attached to it dropped on the spot where he had just been standing. Roger looked up at the hole in the ceiling, and then down at the smashed porcelain strewn across the floor. He sighed again and followed them out.

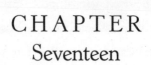

CHAPTER
Seventeen

Roger found himself being shaken out of sleep. Someone was calling his name.

'What?' Roger opened his eyes. He was leaning on the kitchen table, his head resting on his arms. He looked up to see the faces of Lady Goodroom, Maddie and Mossbelly MacFearsome staring back. 'Sorry, I didn't mean to, I just fell asleep.'

'It's all right,' said Lady Goodroom, sitting on a chair and pulling Maddie close to her. 'It's the tension of the whole thing.'

'You will become accustomed,' said Moss, also sitting. 'More fights you have, stronger you become.'

'I'm fine,' said Maddie. 'I'm not sleepy.' She stifled a yawn. 'Well, maybe a little. But I proved that I can fight, didn't I?'

'You were very brave,' said Lady Goodroom, hugging Maddie. 'Very, very brave, but also very foolish. You could have killed yourself.'

'No I couldn't,' said Maddie. 'I know how to drive a tractor. Bet you can't drive one, Rog!'

'How's Lord Goodroom?' asked Roger, ignoring what Maddie had just said.

'He's upstairs,' said Lady Goodroom. 'I've treated him and given him a potion so that he will sleep. It's a rather nasty flesh wound . . .' Her voice tailed off and she began to cry softly. 'When I think that just a tiny bit more to the left and he would be . . .'

Maddie put her arms around her aunt. They held each other.

Moss stood up. 'He'll mend. Do not let a worryworm enter your head.' His voice dropped. 'Now we must plan.'

'Plan what?' asked Lady Goodroom. 'There's nothing we can do. They have the Doomstone Sword *and* the hammer.'

'No,' said Moss. 'I, of course, have the *true* hammer.' He put his right hand under his beard and pulled at the hammer strapped there.

'But,' said Lady Goodroom, 'the one in the—'

'A falsification!' said Moss, waggling the hammer in his hand. 'It was a red rabbit. We are not finished. We still have a chance to smash the Doomstone Sword.'

'I don't understand,' said Lady Goodroom, shaking her head.

'This is the true hammer,' said Moss. 'The one *they* have is a false hammer with no power.'

'You mean . . .' Lady Goodroom hesitated. 'You *lied* to us?'

'Yes,' said Moss, nodding. 'You have the truth of it. A great cunning lie. Unfortunately my plan did not reach fruition, as I could not hand over the true hammer in time to do its work. They attacked too quickly.'

'All that . . .' spluttered Lady Goodroom, 'stuff with me locking it up in the safe . . . *lies?*'

'Of course,' said Moss. 'I did not become Captain of the Royal Guard by my skill in combat alone. I am a fox in cunning. I foresee eventualities and plan accordingly.'

'Like when the gorefiends would attack us,' muttered Roger, who was growing angrier by the minute.

Moss's face darkened under the covering of dust.

Lady Goodroom held up a hand. 'Explain please, Captain. Why you didn't trust us, your friends?'

Moss glared at Roger for a moment before he continued. 'If you had known about the hammer it would now be in the possession of Leatherhead Barnstorm. I hid the true hammer where everyone would have sight of it, and yet would never see it.' He patted his beard and chest. 'Only three were trusted with the real truth.' He tapped the side of his nose, twice.

'*I trusted you!*' Roger shouted furiously, standing up. 'You *asked* me to trust you!'

Moss stood. His face was like thunder. 'What nonsense is this? You had the knowledge! As Destroyer you had to know the whereabouts of the true hammer. My Queen and *you* are the only ones who knew of the great cunning, apart from myself.'

'What are you talking about?' screamed Roger. 'How would I know about your great cunning? You've only just told us, just now!'

'Have you left your brain in a wheelbarrow?' Moss stepped closer to Roger and put his hand on his sword. 'Or is this foul treachery?'

Roger moved closer to Moss and glared back at him. '*You* never told *me* about a false hammer.'

Moss thrust his face forward. His eyes were narrow slits. 'I told you in the spinkie-den. We shared merry-go-down and laughed at my cunning in a most jocular manner.'

Roger leaned forward and looked down. 'No – you – did – not.'

'Yes – I – did.' Moss's face was almost touching Roger's face. 'I showed you the false hammer and gave you the two-nose tap, and let you into the great secret. I also gave you an eye-winker!' Little flecks of spittle flew out of Moss's mouth and landed on Roger. 'You made a joke when I showed to you where the true hammer was hidden.'

'What?' Roger took a step backwards and waved a hand in front of his nose as the dwarf's breath hit him in the face. 'You didn't tell me—'

'Enough!' Lady Goodroom placed herself in front of Moss. 'Both of you! Remember why we are here and what is at stake. You've had problems communicating with each other. There are different ways of expressing things; it's not always clear.' She held up both hands. 'But we are all on the same side. My husband is lying upstairs, gravely wounded.' She stared hard at Moss for a moment. 'We can *discuss* this later. Now sit down. Both. Sit!'

'I'm sitting,' yelled Maddie, pulling out a chair. 'Look at me.' She fussed about, wiping the chair in an exaggerated manner, then plumped herself down in a cloud of dust and looked around. 'There, that's what's called sitting down – it's dead easy. What are we going to do now? Anything sensible? Or are we just going to carry on doing crazy stuff? I don't mind.'

There was silence for a few moments. Roger sat down. Moss also sat down, his nose barely peeping over the table.

'That's better,' said Lady Goodroom. 'Thank you,

Maddie.' She looked at Moss. 'So. We can still break the Doomstone Sword?'

Moss nodded. His face was tight.

'How?' asked Roger, still simmering. 'How are we going to break the blinking sword? Even with the real hammer, where do we go? We don't know where they've gone.'

'Actually, I have an idea where they're going,' said Lady Goodroom. 'Wait here a moment, all of you.' She wagged a finger at them and left the room.

Roger and Moss stared at each other. Maddie looked at both in turn and stuck out her tongue.

'Make room on the table,' said Lady Goodroom, returning with her arms full of rolled maps.

Roger and Moss cleared and wiped the table while Maddie helped Lady Goodroom to spread the maps. They placed pots on the corners to keep them flat.

'This is my area of responsibility,' said Lady Goodroom, waving a hand over the maps. 'What we have to do is decide where they will first go to awaken the ogres.'

'There are many standing stone sites where the ogres sleep,' said Moss. 'They cover all the lands and the islands of the four countries.'

'They could be going anywhere,' said Maddie, scratching at her short hair and releasing a shower of dust. 'There are standing stones all over the place.'

'There are some near here,' said Lady Goodroom. 'Look.' She tapped a map with her finger. 'That's us. It must be within a reasonable distance.'

'Ah, yes,' said Moss, standing on tiptoe to look at the maps. 'But many ogres also sleep in the lands of England and Wales and Ireland. Think of the Great Henge of Salisbury.'

'Yes, yes,' said Lady Goodroom. 'I know, I know. But it doesn't make sense for Leatherhead to travel that far to begin the Awakening. They will start here, and then sweep down the country gathering more dwarves and ogres, getting stronger. Leatherhead found the Doomstone Sword in the south and brought it here. He wanted it here to bring you out, because of that spitting competition.' Lady Goodroom looked at Moss for a few moments before continuing. 'And so I think that I know where they are going . . .'

'How can you know?' asked Moss.

Roger and Maddie leaned their arms on the table and watched.

'You *told* me, Captain Moss,' said Lady Goodroom. 'Remember when we spoke in the library about the Great Frog Gobbing Contest?'

'I have the memory,' said Moss, 'but not the detail.'

Lady Goodroom continued. 'You mentioned the

name of the village where the competition was held – Fowlis Wester – a small village near Crieff, not far from here.'

'So what?' asked Roger, his chin resting in his hands.

'Well,' said Lady Goodroom, going to the map. 'If I'm right, it's where Leatherhead will go to start the Awakening.'

Moss shook his head. 'Sounds roaky to me. You are grasping at a slippery eel.'

Lady Goodroom nodded her head. 'But here's the thing: I know the location of all the standing stones.' She tapped the map. 'It's part of my job to know the exact sites, to make sure they're not disturbed, not built on or anything like that. And Fowlis Wester, here, is one of the sites.' She paused. 'This, I think, is where the ogres will first rise. He will start at the place of his great humiliation. Revenge!'

Maddie clapped her hands. 'Well done, clever Aunty G.'

'It is still—' began Moss.

'I know, I know,' said Lady Goodroom. 'It's not certain, but it's a reasonable assumption? You know him better than anyone, Captain Moss. But even in the short, horrible time I spent with him I got a strong sense of his obsessive hatred and desire for revenge.' She nodded.

131

'The Great Frog Gobbing Contest is where it all started. That's where he'll begin the Awakening. I'm sure I'm right.'

'Hmmm,' said Moss, nodding at Lady Goodroom. 'I fear it may be an angry badger chase, but I have nothing better. Let us go to Fowlis Wester.'

'Thank you,' said Lady Goodroom, and she blew out a long breath. 'Should we leave now?'

'Yes,' said Moss. 'We have a little time to get there. The gorefiends must return to a graveyard. They will begin when it is daylight on the morrow.'

'Right,' said Lady Goodroom. 'It's now a race against time to save the world. Let's get on with it before it's too late.' She pointed at Roger and Maddie. 'You two remain here. Captain Moss, come with me. We have things to do!'

Roger turned back to the table as Lady Goodroom and Moss left the room. He gazed at the map and found his home town, Perth. He placed a finger on it. 'That's where I live,' he said to Maddie, leaning on the table beside him. 'Or at least, that's where I *used* to live.'

Maddie smiled at Roger and whispered back. 'You'll get home again, don't worry.'

'You were very brave,' said Roger. 'I could never have done that. Driving through the doors.'

'I was, wasn't I?' Maddie gave a nervous giggle. 'What a mess, though. And the owner of the tractor won't be very

132

happy when he comes to collect it tomorrow and finds that it's missing.'

Lady Goodroom came back into the room, looking for her car keys. Moss was right behind her. 'Ah, yes,' said Lady Goodroom. 'While we're gone, Maddie, can you tell the farmer who owns that tractor that we'll make sure we pay him back.'

'I won't, because I'm coming with you,' said Maddie, standing up straight and staring determinedly at Lady Goodroom.

'Maddie, you're not—'

'Yes I am!' Maddie spoke very calmly. 'You'd all be dead if it wasn't for me. I got that tractor. I drove it. I saved you. My plan worked. Yours didn't even get started! I am *not* staying behind.'

Roger looked up at Lady Goodroom and Maddie facing each other.

'No, Maddie,' said Lady Goodroom. 'You have to stay here, it's too dangerous.'

'I'm coming with you,' said Maddie. 'And nothing will stop me.'

'But Maddie, dear,' said Lady Goodroom, holding out both hands. 'Uncle Pen. You have to look after him.'

'Put a healing spell on him. That'll keep him safe while we are away. I'll be much more use with you than at home.'

Lady Goodroom looked at Moss and Roger. They both nodded.

'She may be a younghede human,' said Moss, 'but she is no tirly-puffkin.'

Lady Goodroom sighed. 'Fine.' She put her hand on Maddie's shoulder. 'But you must do as you are told. Right, we're leaving in five minutes! Everyone have a quick wash and brush-up.'

As Lady Goodroom and Maddie left the room, Moss stood in front of Roger.

'I thought you had a full understanding of the hammer,' he growled.

'Nope,' said Roger. 'No idea – I just thought we were playing a daft game.'

'*Hummnnumph!*' Moss's face darkened again. 'I do not play . . . daft games!' He muttered under his breath for a few moments before speaking again. 'I forget that most humans are not clever. They are easily pitchkettled. Dwarves have the intelligence. And, of course, merry-go-down had been taken.'

Roger looked up at the ceiling and took a deep breath.

'You know you are still the one who has to break the Doomstone Sword?' Moss asked.

Roger breathed out slowly and looked at the dwarf. 'Why? You could get someone much better than me.'

'No doubt,' said Moss. 'But once I have named a Destroyer, they cannot be un-named. Not until the deed is completed. And my instinct when we first met is right. You are a warrior, Destroyer.'

'I'm not,' said Roger. 'Why can't you just say – *OK, it's not you any more, it's you* – and pick someone else? Who else knows it's me, apart from Lady G, Penrose and Maddie?'

'*I* know!' thundered Moss. 'And a dwarf keeps his word, unlike humans. And I have a reputation for sound judgment. I would rather eat a vanished turnip than have dwarves say I was wrong. *You are the Destroyer.*' He turned round and swept out of the kitchen, trailing dust.

CHAPTER
Eighteen

'It's this way,' said Lady Goodroom, as her old Jaguar saloon left the A9 on the outskirts of Perth and took the road to Crieff. 'We carry on past Methven until we see the sign for Fowlis Wester, then it's on the right.'

Roger sat in the front passenger seat clutching the real hammer in both hands. He was squeezing the hammer so tightly that his hands were tingling. He tried to relax his grip but the tingling was still there. *Perhaps some magic was leaking out?*

Moss and Maddie were in the back of the car. Earlier, when Lady Goodroom had switched on the car radio, Moss had jumped off his seat and banged his head on the roof. He was still muttering and growling, but he had stopped swearing.

Daylight was just beginning to creep over the countryside.

'That's Methven,' said Lady Goodroom, switching off the car lights. 'We're close.'

'There,' said Roger, moments later, pointing at a signpost. 'Fowlis Wester.'

Lady Goodroom slowed down and indicated right.

'Here goes,' said Lady Goodroom. Taking a deep breath, she turned the steering wheel and drove up a narrow road. At the end of the road stood a small village with a red stone standing in the middle of a grassy area.

'Is that—?' began Maddie.

'No, no,' said Lady Goodroom. 'That's a copy of an old stone. We are looking for something much older. Anyway, it's not in the village, it's further out.' She glanced at Roger. 'Should I have stayed with Penrose?'

'No, ladyship,' rumbled Moss from the back of the car. 'We have a task to undertake.'

'As soon as we've broken the Doomstone Sword,' said Maddie, leaning forward and patting Lady Goodroom's shoulder, 'then we'll be home again.'

'Yes,' said Lady Goodroom. 'I know you are right, but—' She sniffed loudly and accelerated through Fowlis Wester.

They continued up a twisting road into the countryside, leaving the village behind them.

'What's that?' asked Roger, pointing left. 'There's a notice there.'

Lady Goodroom stopped beside a low wooden gate

with a chain and a padlock lying beside it. The gate was wide open.

The notice read: *Conservation area – all dogs must be kept on a lead.*

'Look,' hissed Lady Goodroom, pointing. 'There.'

Roger undid his seat belt and wound down his window. In the distance he could see the outlines of two buildings with a large truck standing beside them. Near the truck was a single standing stone and the outlines of several fallen ones some distance away. Small figures were moving around. One of the figures was holding something that shone brightly.

'By the piddling puddocks of Lochranza,' muttered Moss, his face pressed hard against the rear passenger window. 'We are too late. The Awakening has begun.'

'What do we do now?' asked Roger, turning in his seat.

'We attack,' said Lady Goodroom, ramming the car into gear and accelerating through the open gate.

The car shot forward. Roger rocked back in his seat and refastened his seat belt. The car began to bounce along the track, faster and faster. Pheasants, disturbed by the noise and spraying earth, flew out of the heather on either side of the dirt road.

'Look!' Lady Goodroom nodded furiously at the windscreen.

Roger could see Leatherhead Barnstorm standing beside the only upright stone. He was holding the Doomstone Sword and looking in their direction.

'Get ready with the hammer, Roger,' shouted Lady Goodroom. 'I'll aim straight for Leatherhead Barnstorm. You'll only get one chance.'

'OK,' Roger shouted back. He squeezed the hammer in his right fist and felt for the door handle with his left hand.

'May your blow be true,' said Moss from the back seat. 'Go for the sword. I'll destroy gorefiends, and the treacherous butler snort-pig.'

'Go, Roger!' screamed Maddie. 'I'll fight them for you!'

Roger opened the passenger door and held it tightly as the car bucked and swayed . . .

Lady Goodroom swerved off the dirt road on to the grass, aiming the car at Leatherhead Barnstorm . . .

And gorefiends suddenly appeared, jumping out from the heather and gorse bushes. They attacked the car, jabbing at the tyres with their spears.

There was a loud bang as a tyre blew. The car swerved and began to roll over. Everything seemed to spin in slow motion. Small coins rattled against the windscreen and an empty cardboard box hit Roger on the ear.

In fright, he dropped the hammer and let go of the

open door. The hammer bounced out of the car, and there was a terrible grating noise as the passenger door was ripped off. The car smashed down on to its roof and stopped moving.

Roger was totally confused. Something was very wrong but he couldn't quite understand what it was. There was a hissing noise coming from somewhere, and a dripping sound.

'Everyone all right?' asked Lady Goodroom in a muffled voice.

'Th-think so,' said Roger, who was just beginning to realise that he was hanging upside down.

'Wow,' said Maddie. 'That was awesome.'

'Bellringing blazes!' shouted Moss, lying on the inside of the roof. 'What kind of wheeled driver are you? I bash my head more times than I have worrywort soup for my break-of-fast!'

'Not my fault, Captain,' said Lady Goodroom. 'A tyre blew. Gorefiends, I think. And you really should wear your seat belt. Now, I would appreciate it if someone would help me. I think I'm suffocating.'

Roger turned to look at Lady Goodroom. She too was upside down, but all Roger could see was an extremely large, knicker-covered bottom with two stout legs attached. He quickly looked away.

There was a noise from the outside and the remaining car doors were wrenched open. Roger could see the wrong-way-round face of a gorefiend leering at him.

'Soon have you out, sir,' said the gorefiend. 'So sorry that you did not break your neck and die.'

Roger's seat belt was cut and he was hauled, head first, out of the car. He stood breathing deeply for a few moments and then looked over to where Lady Goodroom, Maddie and Moss were being dragged out.

Lady Goodroom was dabbing at her nose with a handkerchief, while Moss was being stripped of his weapons. He had the same stricken look on his face that Roger had seen before – his dwarf friend was obviously once more under the power of the Doomstone Sword.

Maddie, meanwhile, was making faces and sticking out her tongue at the gorefiends surrounding them.

'So, this time you come to me, eh?' Leatherhead Barnstorm walked towards them, the sword leaning on his shoulder. 'Your timing is good. Before you die you will see my triumph.'

'What?' asked Lady Goodroom, pulling at her skirt and staggering slightly as she looked about. 'Where's that cowardly butler? I'm going to do something very nasty to him.'

'Over there,' said Leatherhead, pointing at a valley

in the distance. 'Meeting *my* army. Bringing them to me – and to the Doomstone Sword.'

They all looked towards the valley.

'I don't see anything,' said Maddie.

There was a signal from Leatherhead. Gorefiends prodded Roger and his companions towards the edge of the valley.

'There, human fool,' snarled Leatherhead. 'Look. Do you see the battle lines for war?'

Roger looked again. He could just see two long lines of small figures moving through the tall grass. 'Who are they?'

'The dwarf army,' gasped Moss. 'They are marching to the power of the Doomstone Sword and the destruction of the human race.'

'Can't we stop them?' asked Roger.

'No!' spluttered Moss, staggering closer to Roger. Sweat was running down his face as he tried to resist the sword. 'All dwarves are restrained by the Doomstone Sword spell.' He moved even closer and hissed through his teeth: 'Hammer?'

Roger's head shook a fraction and his eyes flicked towards the upside-down car. Two gorefiends were standing on top of the underside, poking at the exhaust pipe with their spears.

'Get it,' hissed Moss.

142

Maddie, who had been watching the exchange between the two of them, put her fingers in her mouth and gave a piercing whistle. 'Hey, little creeps!' she shouted, sticking her arms out at crazy angles as she started dancing and singing. 'Look what I can do!'

The gorefiends turned to look at the dancing girl.

Roger began to edge sideways towards the burning car . . .

There was a loud *whooomph* as the Jaguar blew up.

A flaming gorefiend shot over Roger's head – it was making an *eeeeeee-hot-hot-hot-eeee* noise as it flew into the valley and exploded in a puff of smoke. The other gorefiend had vanished.

'That didn't go well,' said Maddie. She stopped dancing and pointed at the nearest gorefiend. 'Do you want to fight?'

The gorefiend lunged with its spear, and Maddie quickly jumped back.

'Just try that without your spear,' she challenged, but she kept her distance.

Roger looked at the pillar of smoke. He was desperately trying to remember where he had dropped the hammer. *If it was inside the car . . . But no, wait! Just before the door had been ripped off . . . he was almost positive that it had fallen out on to the grass.*

143

'Look!' yelled Leatherhead, laughing. 'You sent a signal.'

The two lines of marching dwarves were joining up and heading towards the black smoke from the burning car.

Lady Goodroom tut-tutted as she looked at the marching army. 'All of this,' she said, half to herself, 'because of a disgusting spitting game between two bone-headed dwarves.'

Leatherhead waved the Doomstone Sword in the air and screamed aloud: 'Come! Come! Come, my brothers! Join the Sword! The destruction of the human race is now.' He stopped shouting and pointed. 'Look! Look who leads the dwarves of your doom. Queen Gwri.'

The column of dwarves was coming up from the valley out of the long grass. The dwarves were marching two abreast. They were singing.

'Is that Queen Gwri?' Roger pointed at a dwarf in a bright yellow cape who was leading the marchers. She had straw-coloured hair and a neatly trimmed blond beard. 'Her feet . . . are . . . are on back to front.'

'Yes,' sighed Moss. 'My goose-footed beauty, to have such looks *and* back-facing feet. My Queen, I have failed her.' The dwarf put his head in his hands.

'It's a sign of great beauty for dwarves,' said Lady Goodroom, shrugging. 'Can't really see it . . . but each to his own. She is a lovely person, though. I get on very well with her.'

'Who's *that weirdo* talking to?' asked Maddie, pointing at a small group of dwarves gathered around Tobias Undercut at the side of the sloping valley.

'Dwarf wizards,' said Lady Goodroom. 'The most powerful wizards in the Innerland. They protect the battle march with their spells.'

'The dwarves all seem very happy,' said Roger. 'I thought humans were the ones who liked to fight.'

'Dwarves don't get out much,' said Lady Goodroom. 'And don't let Moss kid you – they love fighting, any excuse.'

As the singing dwarves made their way out of the valley, Queen Gwri broke off from the column, walked over to Leatherhead Barnstorm and stopped in front of him.

'You have the Doomstone Sword,' said Queen Gwri, looking directly at Leatherhead.

'I must be obeyed,' agreed Leatherhead.

Queen Gwri stared hard at him. 'Yes,' she said at last. 'What are your commands?'

'We start the war,' said Leatherhead. 'And after the first human blood has been spilled, *you* shall be my bride.'

There was a long pause before Queen Gwri replied, her voice breaking a little as she spoke. 'As the holder of the Doomstone Sword commands. You have won.' There was another pause. She wiped at her eyes. 'But . . . though I know that my attractiveness is great, surely you would not rush me into marriage? Would you not wait for the customary thirty years to pass before we wed?' She pointed a finger at the large wart on the end of her nose. 'I realise that this exquisite birthborn and my backward feet are irresistible, but *please* allow me to mourn. Mossbelly MacFearsome has waited almost thirty years as my betrothed. We were soon to be married.'

'Indeed you are irresistible,' said Leatherhead. Then he pointed at Moss. 'But I am not that blorebated bubblebow! I am *not* waiting thirty years.' Leatherhead lifted the Doomstone Sword from his shoulder. 'I have power, and I'm going to use it.' He muttered and tittered to himself. 'Starting with Mossbelly. He will be the first to die . . . *horribly.*'

'You *do* have the power,' said Gwri. 'All I ask – beg of you – is to stay your hand until after my departure. Spare me the sight of what you are going to do.'

'Your majesty,' shouted Lady Goodroom. 'You can't leave us like this! I have served you well for years.' She pointed at Maddie and Roger. 'They are children. Surely—'

'Silence!' Leatherhead snarled at Lady Goodroom. His little eyes blazed and spittle flew out of his mouth. He turned back to Queen Gwri and pointed at Moss. 'No! I kill him *now*. I have waited too long for this. I must kill him. I swore an oath!' Leatherhead stamped a foot on the grass and then let out a little *eeeeek* scream. He limped around in a circle, stopped and rubbed his injured thigh.

'Mossbelly MacFearsome was my betrothed,' said Queen Gwri, watching Leatherhead closely. 'I cannot see him die. My feelings were strong.' She held up a hand. 'If you agree to my request, I could elevate you beyond consort.'

'But I want to—' Leatherhead stopped rubbing. 'To what? What is "beyond consort"?'

'*King*,' said Queen Gwri.

'King?' Leatherhead limped towards the Queen. 'How can you . . . do that? You can't do that.'

'I can,' said Queen Gwri. 'I can pass a Royal dwarf law in your favour. You would be King. King Leatherhead Barnstorm. And I . . .' Queen Gwri hesitated. 'I would be willing to marry you . . . sooner.'

'I don't need you to be willing, for this sword can make you do my bidding,' thundered Leatherhead. 'Feel its power!' He lifted the Doomstone Sword from his shoulder and pointed at Gwri. Blue sparks danced around the blade and the Queen swayed and clutched at her chest. She staggered back, fell to her knees and then toppled forward on to her hands. She was gasping for breath.

Moss made a sound like he was being strangled, but he couldn't make a move against Leatherhead.

Still crouching and gasping, Queen Gwri raised her head. There were tears running down her face.

'See!' Leatherhead cackled, resting the sword on his shoulder again. 'You do as I command. I am master!'

The Queen trembled and sat back in the grass clutching her stomach as if in great pain. She rocked back and forward, then pulled her cloak tight around her body and looked up. 'But as King your position would be unassailable.' She groaned again. 'You would not even need to have the sword in your possession at all times. You could lock it away safely, and still be supreme ruler.'

Leatherhead raised his foot to stamp it again, but slowly lowered it back down. He thought for a few moments, then shrugged his shoulders. 'King, and marry me in five years, willingly?'

Queen Gwri climbed slowly and carefully to her feet. She dabbed at her eyes with the back of her hand. 'King, and ten years, willingly.'

'King and ten then, we are betrothed!' roared Leatherhead. He pointed at the prisoners. 'Gorefiends, after I have taken the Queen away from here, kill all of them. Fulfil *my* oath on *my* orders. Oh, and bring me Mossbelly's head. I'll cut the top off, scoop it out, and keep my baccy pipe in it.' He stood in front of Moss and stared at him. 'I hate you,' he said, spitting out the words. 'I've dreamed of this moment for a long, long time. You will be dead in the shortest time. But not by my hand.' He raised the Doomstone Sword in the air. 'So this will have to suffice until they separate your head from your body.'

The sword whistled through the air and sliced off a small tuft of hair at the end of Moss's beard.

'Aaaaanguinnginghumm!' Moss stood, deep purple with rage, every part of him trembling with suppressed fury.

Leatherhead threw back his head and roared with laughter. 'I'll do some more! This I like!'

'Please,' said Queen Gwri, tears dripping into her beard. 'Enough! Please! You have everything you want. Please, no more, I beg you.' She raised an arm and pointed at Moss. Her voice was shaky as she spoke. 'My heart, which you owned for so long, now lies broken – in the *dirt*.' Her pointing finger swung out and down a little. 'We are over. Farewell.'

Moss stood perfectly still, all the anger draining out of him. He gave the Queen the slightest of nods.

Queen Gwri looked directly at Leatherhead. 'Please.'

Leatherhead waved the point of the sword in front of Moss's face, and then he shrugged. 'Very well,' he said, giggling. He looked at the gorefiends surrounding the prisoners. 'When you bring me his head, cut off his beard, I'll smoke it in my pipe.'

'Men, eh,' said Maddie quietly. 'What are they like? Stupid.'

'Be quiet,' whispered Lady Goodroom. 'Don't speak. Just be ready.'

'For what?' hissed Roger. He looked anxiously at Lady Goodroom and Maddie. Both seemed remarkably calm.

Lady Goodroom did not answer. Maddie smiled, winked at Roger, and raised a clenched fist.

To the side, row after row of dwarfs were forming up; all wore armour and carried weapons: swords, axes, spears, shields and two-headed hammers.

'Now,' said Leatherhead, still burbling away. 'There is a great thing to be done.' He walked to the only upright standing stone and raised the Doomstone Sword above his head. He plunged the sword deep into the rock, then pulled it out and marched over to the other stones scattered flat on the ground and began cutting into them.

'What's he doing that for?' asked Roger.

Before anyone could answer him, the ground around the upright standing stone split open. Gorse, heather and earth erupted as two giant hands appeared, clawing at the sky. A massive head and body sat up, ripping the earth apart, then the giant – a female – yawned and stretched and began picking at the soil and rock clinging to her face.

CHAPTER
Nineteen

'She's huge,' gasped Roger, looking up at the massive, hideous face with two large teeth protruding from the bottom jaw.

'Yes,' said Lady Goodroom. 'You knew the ogres were giants?'

'No,' whispered Roger, barely able to get the word out.

'Did Moss not tell you?' asked Lady Goodroom, shielding her eyes as she watched the ogress. 'She's big, but I've heard that the Salisbury ones are *really* big.'

Roger shook his head, unable to speak.

The giant ogress stood up. '*Nnn-aaa-ahh,*' rumbled across the heather. '*Iss it time to rise?*' She yawned again and looked around as chunks of earth and boulders cascaded down from her body. Then the ogress sneezed. A huge blob of liquid shot out of her nose and hit the front row of dwarves, knocking several of them off their feet.

'*Oh, it's fighting, is it?*' The ogress sniffed several

times and wiped her face with the back of her hand. '*Sorry, somefin' stuck up me nose.*'

The dwarves got to their feet and began to wipe at the secretions dripping from their bodies.

'Come!' Leatherhead waved the Doomstone Sword in the air. 'It is time to destroy the faithless race.'

More giants began to rise from under their fallen stones. The smallest was huge and the biggest gigantic. There were two absolutely enormous ones – the first to waken, and a second even bigger one. The second one looked around and then stamped his foot, causing several rows of dwarves to raise their shields as protection from flying earth and rock.

'*Who knocked my stone down? Who knocked all the stones down?*' he demanded in a low rumble.

'Humans,' yelled Leatherhead. 'No respect do they have for the old ways, and they have desecrated your places of sleep. We have been forgotten. Poison is poured on the earth and all warnings ignored. They are a stupid, dangerous race. Many ages ago, we made an agreement, we dwarves, you ogres and others. And now the time is here – time to end the human race.'

Just as Leatherhead stopped speaking something dark shot out of the torn earth and sped into the sky.

'What's *that*?' Roger pointed.

'Watch,' said Lady Goodroom, as the thing turned and glided back down. It flapped its wings and then soared again.

'It's . . . it's . . .' Roger struggled to speak.

'It's a dragon,' said Lady Goodroom. 'Look – there are more of them! Did the captain not mention dragons?'

'N-no, he didn't,' said Roger.

'They're beautiful,' gasped Maddie, as she watched the aerial display above. 'I want one.'

More dragons appeared. One, a deep turquoise with a greyish stomach, sent a blast of fire streaming to the ground. The gorse and heather burst into flames. Other dragons followed, gliding down and pouring out their fiery breath. Black smoke curled in the air from the scorched earth.

Lady Goodroom shook her head. 'Magnificent creatures, aren't they? They're warming themselves up. They belong to the ogres, sort of pets.'

Roger, mesmerised, watched as the dragons soared and dived above him.

A horn sounded: five long blasts. The dwarf army began to move again.

Leatherhead Barnstorm walked back to Queen Gwri and stood in front of her. 'Come, my betrothed,' he said, holding out his hand. 'We'll lead the army together.'

The Queen bowed slightly. 'You have the Doomstone Sword and the hammer. Lead as you will, my future King.'

'Betrothed,' said Leatherhead, chuckling as he took the Queen's hand. He began to shout orders. More horns sounded, drums began to beat, dwarf banners were unfurled, flapping and cracking in the wind.

The giant ogres lumbered over to some trees and pulled them out of the ground. They ripped off the branches and then began to thump the tree trunks into the ground to the beat of the drums.

'Please remember,' said Queen Gwri. 'Not until they are out of the sight of my eyes. Nor do I want to hear their agonised screams.'

Leatherhead nodded and began shouting orders at the gorefiends. A group of them quickly scampered over to the four captives and raised their spears.

With a last hateful, lingering look at Moss, Leatherhead – still holding the Queen's hand – walked away, with the rest of the gorefiends following.

The prisoners stood, quietly watching, until the last of the dwarf army had disappeared into the long grass.

Released from the power of the sword, Moss staggered forward, almost on to the tips of the gorefiend's spears. 'Don't kill me!' he cried, falling to his knees and crawling about aimlessly. He looked up at the nearest gorefiend. 'I was only doing what I was told, obeying orders. You can't end me, I'm too young.'

'Oh, I like this,' said the gorefiend as Moss continued to crawl, moving in small circles.

The gorefiends began to snigger and chatter.

'Not so bold now, Captain.'

'You lost courage, Captain?'

'Soon be dead, Captain.'

Roger looked around nervously and moved closer to Lady Goodroom. He couldn't believe what he was seeing, the way Moss was behaving.

Lady Goodroom smiled, her teeth tightly clenched. 'Get weddy, Wodger,' she muttered.

'What for?' Roger whispered.

'Here we go,' said Maddie, taking up a fighting position.

'Stop!' The gorefiend in front of Moss held up a claw. 'This is not correct behaviour. The Queen's champion would not do this. This is a trick.'

The gorefiends began muttering to each other.

'Trick.'

'Queen's champion.'

'Not correct behaviour.'

The gorefiend waved its claw excitely. 'He is looking

for something. Something on the ground.' There was a moment's silence. 'A weapon! He's searching for a weapon.'

The group of gorefiends quickly formed a tight circle around the kneeling dwarf, every spear pointing at his body.

'You are going to die,' said the first gorefiend. 'No chitter-chatter, just die. Ready, brothers?'

The other gorefiends moved closer and Moss winced as some of the spear tips touched him.

'Kill him – now!' screeched the gorefiend.

Just then, Lady Goodroom farted.

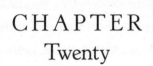

CHAPTER
Twenty

It was the loudest fart Roger had ever heard.

'Pardon me,' said Lady Goodroom. 'I'm a little . . . flatulent today, from all the excitement.'

The gorefiends surrounding Moss lowered their spears and looked at Lady Goodroom.

'Do that again,' said a gorefiend. It walked over and prodded a claw at Lady Goodroom's stomach. The other gorefiends were twitching their noses, sniffing the air.

'Do it again!' said the gorefiend.

'I can't just—' Lady Goodroom staggered as more gorefiends joined in, pushing at her stomach with their claws. 'I'm not a machine—'

'Do it!'

'Make noise like trumpet!'

'Will you leave me alone?' Lady Goodroom slapped at the claws digging into her.

There was a deep growling sound, like a very angry

dwarf trying to clear several small boulders from the back of his throat.

The gorefiends turned to see what the noise was.

Captain Mossbelly MacFearsome was making the noise. He was standing upright holding two small axes, and there was a ferocious look on his face.

'King Golmar's Braces!' yelled Moss. He ran at the nearest gorefiend and, with a swipe, cut it in half.

'Wasn't expecting that,' said the gorefiend, as it toppled over.

Moving at speed, Moss killed two more gorefiends. Lady Goodroom pushed Roger to one side and threw herself forward. She hit the ground, rolled on to her left shoulder and came up holding a small spear.

Moss roared as he tore into the creatures.

Maddie twisted her body around and leaped into the air, swinging her foot at the nearest gorefiend. Her kick connected and the gorefiend went tumbling over, its spear flying out of its claws.

Maddie dropped to the ground in a crouch and then straightened up and turned to Lady Goodroom. 'Did you see that, Aunt Gwen?' she shouted. 'It worked, it really worked!'

Roger grabbed a gorefiend just as it was about to stick its spear in Maddie's back. He pulled the gorefiend by the shoulders and shoved it away. Lady Goodroom whipped around and thrust her spear into the gorefiend's chest. It collapsed in a cloud of smoke.

Roger lifted a fallen spear as two gorefiends closed in on him. One lunged forward, aiming at his head. He knocked the spear aside and jabbed the gorefiend in the shoulder. He turned to face the other one – and tripped. Both jumped forward, spears raised ready to stab him.

There was a soft swishing sound. The gorefiends' heads flew off. Their remains collapsed, yellow smoke rising from their bodies.

Mossbelly MacFearsome walked into view, sheathing his axes. He held out a hand to Roger. 'Well fought. You are getting better at battling. A few more and you'll be challenging myself for Queen's champion, eh?'

Roger shook his head as he was helped to his feet. He couldn't speak.

'You all right?' Lady Goodroom appeared, red-faced. Roger nodded and looked around. All that remained of the gorefiends was a nasty smell and some yellow marks on the gorse and heather.

Maddie stood beside her aunt and looked at Roger. 'Thank you,' she said, smiling. 'You saved me. Warrior. Destroyer.' Then she stuck out her tongue.

Roger licked his lips. 'What happened? I thought that we were—'

'This clever human woman,' said Moss, pointing at Lady Goodroom. He stepped back, put his hands on his hips and looked up at her admiringly. 'She knew gorefiends could not resist an emission of intestinal gas – and one of such powerful magnificence – for they have fascination for all bodily functions.'

'I didn't . . .' Lady Goodroom's eyes blinked rapidly and her face grew even redder. 'That is . . . I mean . . . I couldn't help . . . I was . . . excited. My digestion is . . .'

'Perfect!' Moss grinned. 'Your wind-breaking is a lion roaring in deep cavern. Magnificent!'

Lady Goodroom gazed at the ground and shook her head; there was a slight smile on her face.

Roger looked at the dwarf. 'How did you get those weapons?'

'My Queen placed weapons in the grass when she fell to her knees,' said Moss. 'That bubbling lickspiggot you saw was not *my* beloved Queen. What you saw was an act of great skill to outwit those fopdoodles.' He laughed. 'But I knew! *And* – she even pointed to the location of the axes, right in front of that waghalter's wink-a-peeps. I, of course, also used *my* considerable acting talent to fool the gorefiends.' He clapped his hands. 'Now, let us get the

161

hammer from the burning carriage area. We must follow the battle march. We still have the smallest of chances if we move with an abundance of speed.' He looked at Lady Goodroom. 'They will attack the nearest large town.'

Lady Goodroom nodded. 'That'll be Perth.'

Roger clenched his fists to stop his hands trembling. Perth was his home – where his mum and little sister were.

The Jaguar car was still burning as Roger, Maddie, Moss and Lady Goodroom approached.

'Maddie, dear,' said Lady Goodroom. 'Go and look in that truck over there. See if Barnstorm and Tobias left the keys in it. We'll look for the hammer.'

'OK,' said Maddie, scampering over the heather towards the truck.

'Where did you drop the hammer, Roger?' asked Lady Goodroom, shielding her face from the heat.

'I had it in my right hand,' said Roger. 'I was holding the car door open with my left and I let go of everything when the car rolled. But I'm fairly sure I saw it fall out.' He looked at Lady Goodroom and then dropped his eyes. 'I'm sorry I let it go. I thought I was going to die.'

Lady Goodroom hugged Roger to her large bosom. 'So did I, Roger. I thought I was going to die too. I was very frightened.' She released him and held him at arm's length. 'Don't tell anyone.'

'I won't.' Roger nodded.

'Come on, then,' said Lady Goodroom, and she began searching the flattened grass where the car had rolled. 'Let's hope the hammer did fall out of the car.'

Roger and Moss joined the search.

'Oh, and Roger,' said Lady Goodroom, pulling at broken heather. 'Something else very important.'

'What?' asked Roger, looking up.

'Don't ever tell anyone that you saw my knickers, or what happened, you know.' Lady Goodroom jerked her head. 'Back there. Promise?'

'I promise,' said Roger, trying not to laugh.

'Do not talk of knickers,' said Moss. 'We are interested in the location of the hammer, not knickers.' He searched on, muttering to himself: 'Undergarments are not for discussion when we are questing.'

'Doors locked,' said Maddie, arriving back. 'Climbed up and looked in, but couldn't see any keys. I could smash the window, but I don't think they're inside.'

'No,' said Lady Goodroom. 'It was a long shot.'

Just then, a glint of something metallic in one of the

bushes near the torn-off car door caught Roger's eye. He slipped his hand into the bush and lifted out the hammer.

'Got it!' he shouted. He felt an enormous sense of relief.

'Well done,' said Lady Goodroom.

'Yes, well done, Roger,' said Moss, taking the hammer from Roger and examining it thoroughly before handing it back. 'Now we follow the battle march and attempt to destroy the Doomstone Sword, again.'

Lady Goodroom blew out her cheeks and sighed. 'I'm not sure that I could walk that far, Captain. It looks pretty rough-going. Thought the truck would have been easier for us.'

'We must go,' said Moss. 'We cannot end the quest to save human race. Once Perth is destroyed and human blood is spilled, there is no way to stop what follows.'

'I know,' said Lady Goodroom, pointing vaguely. 'It is just that I'm a little too short of breath to walk over all that, never mind catch up with them.'

'I'll help you,' said Maddie. 'You can lean on me if you like.'

'Thank you, dear,' said Lady Goodroom. 'Not sure that I'll get very far, though.'

'I've got an idea,' said Roger.

They all looked at Roger.

'Why don't we walk back to where we came in,' continued Roger, 'and take the road down to Fowlis Wester, then the main road. It's not that far and it's nearly all downhill and it's not grass. Once we're at the main road we could get a lift. If we're very lucky we might be in Perth before the giants and dwarves.'

Lady Goodroom and Moss MacFearsome looked at each other.

'Yes,' said Moss. 'Good. We go, now.'

'Clever Roger,' said Maddie, and she punched him on the arm.

'Thanks,' said Roger, frowning and rubbing his arm.

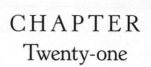

CHAPTER
Twenty-one

When they reached the road, Roger could see four children facing him beside the open gate. Four bikes were propped against the gateposts.

'Hello, children,' shouted Lady Goodroom. 'Nice day.'

There was no reply from the two boys and two girls.

'Out for a cycle in the countryside on a lovely Sunday?' yelled Lady Goodroom in an even louder voice. She glanced at her watch. 'You'll be going for lunch soon. I wonder if you would do us a small favour before you go?'

The children did not speak. They stood absolutely still. Their eyes were wide and their faces were pale.

'Well, this is nice,' said Lady Goodroom, stopping in front of the children. 'I'm Gwendolena. This is my friend, Moss. And this is Maddie, and Roger – they are children, like yourselves, well, maybe a little older.'

'Can we borrow your bikes?' Maddie asked quickly.

The children did not move.

'Can we, *please*, borrow your bikes?' asked Roger.

'We only need them for a short time. We'll give them back.'

The children did not speak. They just stood staring blankly at the sky.

'Answer!' snarled Moss.

One of the girls slowly raised her hand and pointed. 'Gi-gi-giants,' she stuttered. 'I saw giants.'

'Drag-on-ons,' said one boy, trembling. 'I saw . . .'

'Dwaffs!' said the other, younger boy, smiling happily. 'Millions and millions of dwaffs.'

'What about dwarves?' Moss stepped closer and gripped his axes.

'*I've wet my pants!*' shrieked the last girl, and she turned, ran down the path and vanished round the corner. The other children scampered after her.

'Stupid, ugly human children,' said Moss as he watched the last child disappear.

'Why are *you* always calling *us* ugly?' Roger spun round and glared at the dwarf. '*We* are not ugly. *You* are ugly.'

'Ugly?' Moss looked bewildered. 'Us? You must be lunar. You are an ugly race with your smooth, bland outer skin. You lack character. You have nothing on your faces, just ugly plainness.'

'Listen, you!' shouted Roger. 'I've had enough from a wizened little prune like you. Just shut up about us being ugly!' He paused for a moment, and then shoved a finger furiously in the dwarf's direction. 'You can't even explain things properly! And you talk gibberish most of the time. You say stupid words!' Roger took a deep breath. 'They were going to kill me back there! But you couldn't help because of a stupid sword, with its stupid powers. You're worse than us humans – much worse!'

'Do not dare to call the Doomstone Sword stupid!' snarled Moss, pointing a stubby finger back at Roger. 'And you did not assist when I was buried under the castle roof!'

'I tried,' roared Roger. 'And I saved you from getting an axe in your head, by stabbing Leatherhead in the leg!'

'I pushed you to safety when the top of the room fell on you,' bellowed Moss.

'That's enough!' said Lady Goodroom, stepping between the shouting boy and dwarf. 'From both of you. Again! Are you mad? We have a job to do. Stop this stupidity at once. Different is not ugly. It's just different. Now, pick a bicycle and be quiet, or I'll smack both your bottoms.'

Glowering at each other, Roger and Moss picked out two bikes. Lady Goodroom chose the largest. Maddie took the last and moved over to stand beside Roger.

'Oh, what a temper you've got, Roger,' she whispered

out of the corner of her mouth. She giggled. 'Standing up to the dwarf champion! I'm going to call you *Rog the Destroyer*.' She clasped her hands under her chin and fluttered her eyelashes. 'My hero,' she sighed.

'Don't call me Rog,' said Roger, still angry but trying not to laugh. 'My name is Roger. And I'm not getting any braver. He just gets me so mad, sometimes. And stop doing that, it's not funny.'

Maddie laughed. 'Roger the Mad Warrior, then. But you're still *my hero*.'

'Maddie!' said Lady Goodroom. 'Behave! Don't tease Roger.' She straddled her child-sized bike, with a little difficulty. 'Right,' she said, when all four were astride their bikes. 'Moss, you go first, then Roger, then Maddie. Make sure you keep your brakes on down the steep part. When we get to the village we'll leave the bicycles and walk the next bit. Off you go, Captain.'

Moss took his feet off the ground and held them out to the side, away from the pedals. He moved forward, began to wobble, gained speed, wobbled again and began to head downhill.

'*Steer*,' screamed Lady Goodroom.

'Watch the ditch!' yelled Maddie.

Moss's front wheel dropped into the ditch at the side of the road. The bike swung up, throwing Moss out of the saddle, and spinning into the air. There was an anguished howl as he crashed through some bushes and disappeared.

Roger, Maddie and Lady Goodroom dropped their bikes and ran down the road.

'There he is,' yelled Maddie, who was the first to arrive at the fallen bike. 'In there.'

'Captain!' yelled Lady Goodroom. 'Captain! Are you all right?'

'Moss!' shouted Roger. 'Mossy!'

Mossbelly MacFearsome was lying on his stomach in the middle of some bracken. He groaned, rolled on to his back and tried to sit up. His face was scratched, his clothing was torn and there was a small branch hanging from his beard.

'What's a prune?' he asked, picking thorns out of his face and body. 'Why did you call me a prune?'

'It's a plum with the juice squeezed out,' said Roger, as he and Maddie clambered into the bushes and helped the dwarf to stand up.

'Ah,' said Moss, gingerly feeling his body and legs. 'Then you are a plum.' He stopped and pointed at Roger's face. 'A smooth shiny plum.'

'Right,' said Roger, and he paused before speaking again. 'You can't ride a bicycle, can you?'

'No,' said Moss.

'You—' said Lady Goodroom, standing on the road, watching. 'You could have been *killed*. Why didn't you say?'

'If *you* can do the bi-cycle, *I* can do the bi-cycle.' Moss shrugged off his helpers, walked back to his bike and picked it up.

'No,' said Roger, lifting his own bike. 'Don't be stupid. Come and sit behind me on the saddle. I'll stand on the pedals and steer.'

'I'll do my own bi-cycle,' said Moss.

'Oh,' said Lady Goodroom, 'for goodness' sake, stop this at once. Get on the back of Roger's bike, now!'

Moss dropped the bike and stood grumbling to himself, picking at things on his face and beard. He walked over and sat on the saddle of Roger's bicycle. The bike creaked and the tyres flattened.

'Hang on tight,' said Roger, pushing hard on the pedals. The bike wobbled and then gathered speed as it moved downhill.

Moss grabbed Roger round the waist and muttered: 'Plum.'

'Prune,' said Roger, braking at the first corner.

'Move along, children,' said Lady Goodroom, as she and Maddie pedalled past them. Lady Goodroom's legs were sticking out to the side and Roger could hear ominous groaning and rumbling noises as she swept past. He was unsure if the sounds were from the bike, or from Lady Goodroom.

They arrived at Fowlis Wester and left the bicycles beside the red stone. Roger's bike had a slightly bent front wheel and two flat tyres. Moss left four little piles of golden stones beside the three bikes.

After a short walk they reached the main road running between Crieff and Perth.

'Now all we need to do is get a lift,' said Lady Goodroom. She looked up the road. 'And here it comes now.'

A bus was trundling along the road towards them, the sign on the front said PERTH. Lady Goodroom held out her hand and the bus slowed down.

Just as the bus began to pull up, the driver leaned forward in his seat and stared out of his windscreen. There was an incredulous look on his face. He sat back again and the bus began to accelerate. Roger, Maddie and Moss shouted and waved, but the bus sped off.

'What is the problem?' said Moss furiously. 'Why did that human not allow us to board his carriage? Is he dumpling-headed?'

Roger turned to look at the dwarf. Moss's face was

covered in dried blood, his beard and hair looked like an explosion in an old mattress, and his clothes were torn. He was hopping about on the pavement waving an axe at the accelerating bus.

'Put that away,' said Roger, pointing at the weapon. 'No one will stop if they see that. And hide yourself behind Lady Goodroom.'

'Why?' asked Moss.

'Be quiet,' said Lady Goodroom, stepping in front of Moss. 'Here comes a car. Let me try again.' She waved her thumb in the air.

The car slowed – and then accelerated away as Moss's head poked out from behind Lady Goodroom. More cars appeared. All did the same thing. As soon as the drivers saw Moss close up, they would quickly accelerate away.

'It's no use,' said Lady Goodroom, pulling out a mobile phone. 'I'm going to phone for a taxi.'

A white van came into view. Lady Goodroom raised a hand and waggled her thumb half-heartedly. The van began to slow. The driver leaned forward and stared through the windscreen.

Then the van stopped.

The driver's door opened and a thin man with tattooed arms jumped out and stood looking at them.

'It's that funny man,' said Maddie quietly. 'The one

who brings our paper towels. He's the one who smashed our fence.'

'Hello there,' said Wullie. 'I was just on my way tae Auchterbolton Castle with a delivery. You'll be needing extra after the do yesterday.' He looked carefully at the four figures. 'Are you needing a lift somewhere?'

'Ah,' said Moss. 'It is a happy meeting to see you again, Wullie.'

'Nice to see you again, wee man,' said Wullie, walking forward and shaking hands with the dwarf.

'Hello, Wullie,' said Roger, smiling. 'Nice to see you.'

Wullie turned to Roger. 'And you as well . . . ?'

'Roger.'

'Aye, Roger, right.'

Wullie looked at Lady Goodroom. 'Hello again, your mamship. I've got your delivery in the van? Special Sunday service for my special customer.' He rubbed his hands together. 'Eh, when I was at your games thingy yesterday, I met the boy and . . . what's his name, the wee fella. He gave me some gold.'

'How did you get that dent in the front of your van?' asked Maddie, pointing. 'Is that a bit of wood caught in the bumper?'

'Eh . . . Oh . . .' Wullie glanced back at his van and shrugged his shoulders. He held out his hand to Lady

174

Goodroom. 'Nice tae see you, your ladymam. Hope you're keeping well?'

Lady Goodroom shook hands with Wullie.

'Would you have interest in more gold?' asked Moss.

'Ah surely would, wee man.' Wullie let go of Lady Goodroom's hand and looked at Moss. 'You're looking a bit rough, son. You're all looking a bit rough. *Ahem*, what would I have tae do for some more gold?'

'The human race is in the most grave danger,' said Lady Goodroom. 'Ogres have been awakened by a malignant gnome called Leatherhead Barnstorm. He has the Doomstone Sword and control of all the dwarves and ogres. He is marching on Perth. It will be destroyed. You've got to help us.'

'Wullie,' said Moss, 'I am Mossbelly MacFearsome, Captain of the Royal Guard. If you do not aid us with transport, my Queen will wed another. Only the hammer the boy carries can defeat him. You must save my Queen from a fate worse than being consumed alive by a gundygut.'

'Oh a-y-e,' said Wullie very slowly, nodding in a knowing manner. 'Righto. Mossybelly, eh? That's a right . . . ehm, a right grand name, so it is.'

'I think you owe us something,' said Maddie, waggling a finger at the front of the van and doing a pretend whistle. 'For a broken fence.'

175

Wullie made a face at Maddie and then turned to Roger.

Roger shrugged his shoulders. 'There's dragons and hundreds of singing dwarves and gorefiends and wizards and lots more.'

'Will you help us, William?' asked Lady Goodroom.

'There will be great danger,' said Moss. 'Our lives could be ended. We could easily be killed dead to the ground.'

Wullie looked at the anxious faces staring at him. He stroked his chin in an exaggerated manner, thought for a few seconds and then said: 'Aye, nae bother. What do you want me tae do?'

CHAPTER
Twenty-two

'So, let me see if I've got this straight,' said Wullie, as they drove towards Perth. 'I've to drive you through an army of dwarves and dragons and giants until I see a bad wee man with a big sword. Then the boy here, Roger, is going to break this sword and you're all gonny give the ladymamship's butler and the bad wee man an awfy doing?'

'Ehm, more or less,' said Lady Goodroom, trying to manoeuvre her arms into a more comfortable position. 'They shot my husband, you know.'

'Aye,' said Wullie grimly, throwing the van round a corner. 'So you said. I like his lordmanship, hope he's all right.' He gave a little laugh and shook his head. 'You've got me as daft as you lot.' He glanced down at Moss. 'And how about you, Mossyman? You're from the underground, you say. Is there lots of gold there?'

'Gold is not an important issue,' said Moss. 'My Queen Gwri and the human race are only things to be thought about.'

'Maybe for you, Mossyman,' said Wullie. 'But I could fair do with some gold before they take you away and lock you up.'

'Wullie,' growled Moss. 'It is not fadoodle I tell you. All I say is true.'

'Aye, right,' said Wullie, glancing at Roger, who was wedged between Moss and the handbrake. 'And how about you, son? You're going to attack a dwarf nutjob who's surrounded by dozens of wild wee men and giants and flying beasties?'

'I'll help him,' said Maddie, stuck tight between her aunt and Moss.

Roger was silent for a few seconds. 'When you put it like that, it doesn't sound like a very good plan, does it?'

'No, no,' said Wullie quickly. 'It's a great plan! One of the best plans I've ever heard. You're all as mad as mince. But it's a great plan! If there's gold, I love your plan.' He banged the steering wheel hard with his hands. 'Wullie saves the world. What a laugh. Wait till ah tell the weans.'

As they reached the bypass overlooking Perth, Lady Goodroom pointed to the side of the road. 'Now, stop here. I don't see anything yet. I think we've got here first.'

Wullie pulled in and stopped on the hard shoulder. He turned and looked at Lady Goodroom.

'Take us to the other side of the road,' said Lady

Goodroom, waving circles in the air with a finger. 'We want to look down towards Perth, see what's happening there. And if we are first we can see them coming down the hills on the other side.'

'Are you sure?' asked Wullie. 'There's an awfy lot of traffic about.'

Lady Goodroom leaned round and shook her head at Wullie. Roger could see her chins were still moving after her head had stopped. 'My good man, we are about to see giants and dragons on this road any second now. Do not worry about some traffic.'

'Oh aye, right, missus,' said Wullie, laughing. 'Ah forgot about the giants and dragons.' He put the gear lever into first and then pressed the indicator for a right turn.

The van pulled out, crossed the two lanes and swung round. An articulated lorry thundered past, horn blaring.

'There,' said Wullie, pulling on the handbrake. 'That you happy now?'

'No,' said Lady Goodroom, looking very pale.

'Phew-eee,' said Maddie.

'Whistling toadstools,' muttered Moss.

'Could you not have looked first?' asked Roger.

'Ah did!' said Wullie. 'You were in nae danger. Well, maybe just a wee bitty. Anyway, tell me, Mossyman, where do you get your gold from? It's a great trick.'

'It is not trickery,' said Moss. 'All dwarves can, if they wish, change stone to gold. It is a thing of great simplicity. All you have to do is—'

Suddenly the sky went dark.

'What in the name—' Wullie stopped talking as an enormous dragon glided down and landed on the carriageway. It flapped its wings several times, then settled and looked around. Fire trickled from the sides of its massive jaws and dripped on to the road.

'Oooh,' moaned Wullie. 'I thought you were all raving nutcases. I was only after the gold.'

'Don't move,' hissed Moss. 'Turn the power off. It's scouting for targets.'

'It's awfy big,' said Wullie, as he switched off the engine and tried to hide behind the steering wheel.

'That one wasn't with them when they left Fowlis Wester,' Roger whispered, sliding lower in his seat.

'No,' said Lady Goodroom. 'It's new. They're gathering as they march. Oh, and look at that.' She pointed to the hills. Several ogres were coming into view. They were striding down, their massive feet slamming into the earth, smashing hedges and fences and kicking over stone walls. Behind them marched the dwarf army with Leatherhead Barnstorm and Queen Gwri at the front.

'Actually, Ah need tae go,' said Wullie, undoing his

seat belt. 'Ah've tae see the dentist – today! All day! He's taking my teeth oot.'

'Good, Wullie!' said Moss. 'Humorous bantering is a sign of a true warrior.'

'I'm no joking, ya wee bam-pot,' said Wullie.

'Look!' Maddie raised her hand and pointed.

A small car was coming along the carriageway. It screeched to a halt and smoke poured from its tyres as it reversed at speed. The dragon's head turned and its eyes glittered, then the dragon lifted its head and breathed out a pillar of flame. The car, tyres still squealing and paint blistering on the bonnet, shot back and crashed into another car. The driver's door in the small car opened and a man got out. He ran across the road and threw himself over the crash barrier into a drainage ditch. Two men got out of the second car, scampered over the road and jumped into the same ditch.

More cars drove up, some tried to reverse and some tried to turn. The panicking motorists crashed into each other, blocking the road.

As the first of the ogres arrived on the dual carriageway, the great dragon flapped its wings and took off, flying towards a nearby football stadium. It circled the stadium, then swooped down. Fire shot out of the dragon's mouth and the stadium building erupted in flames. The dragon circled again, as if inspecting its work, and then flew back and landed beside an ogre, who patted and tickled it under its chin.

People were coming out of the houses around the burning stadium. They ran about shouting and pointing at the giant ogres and dwarf army gathering in the fields and on the road.

The dwarves were lining up now in tight parade-ground squares. Ogres moved into the spaces between the squares, while dwarf wizards were positioning themselves beyond the outer squares. They were shouting and waving their arms in the air.

'Spells,' said Moss. 'The Indestructabubble is forming. The dragons are flying to a safe height. We must move!'

Dragons flew over the dwarf army and climbed at colossal speed before disappearing into the clouds.

'What's a—?' Roger started.

'Wullie!' yelled Moss. 'Move your carriage forward at once! At a fast pace, but slowly. We must be under the Indestructabubble, or we die. Go!'

Wullie started his van, muttering to himself. 'Go fast, slowly. What's that about?'

A deep rumble of thunder shook Wullie's van as it crept along the road. Rain began to splash against the windscreen and rattle on the roof. Black clouds tumbled across the sky, then lightning flickered briefly, and moments later a louder peal of thunder boomed overhead.

'Go further, Wullie, quickly!' shouted Moss, waving a hand in a forward motion while peering through the windscreen. 'The bubble is closing!'

'I can't see anything,' said Roger, staring through the same windscreen.

'Use your wink-a-peeps!' Moss pointed a finger. '*There!*'

Roger squinted hard. Then he saw it. A massive translucent bubble was forming in the sky. The top of the bubble was already there and the sides were rapidly falling towards the ground. Any moment now, the bubble would close up.

'*Go!*' shrieked Moss.

The van sped forward, faster and faster. It slipped under the bubble just a second before the sides completed their descent and thumped into the ground.

'Halt your carriage!' Moss slapped a hand on the instrument panel. 'Now!'

Wullie stamped on the brake pedal, and the van skidded to a halt. He pulled on the handbrake. 'Can you no' make up yer mind—'

Thunder boomed overhead and the sky lit up as lightning bolts streaked down.

Everyone in the van, except Moss, ducked.

'Fear not,' shouted Moss, as thunder rolled across the sky. 'We are safely inside the Indestructabubble. Just!'

'Oh my!' Wullie gripped the steering wheel tightly. 'What in the name o' the . . . What's happening?'

'The war,' said Moss. 'It begins.'

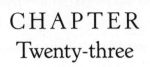

CHAPTER
Twenty-three

Thunder hammered Roger's eardrums. A bolt of lightning hurtled down directly above the dwarves. It hit the top of the Indestructabubble, showering sparks into the air and cascading down the sides.

'Ooooh . . .' said Wullie. 'Would you look at that?' He reached to switch off the engine, but Moss slapped his hand away.

The dwarves were unharmed. The massive, transparent half-bubble was covering the dwarf army and the surrounding area.

Moss looked around. 'Sound judgment, we are safe here. But keep the combustion engine on.'

'Safe?' Wullie glared at Moss, and then pointed through the windscreen. 'Are you mad? Have you seen what's out there?'

'How can that be?' gasped Roger. 'How can *that* keep out lightning?'

'It stops everything,' said Moss. He jumped down from the seat. 'Nothing can penetrate the Indestructabubble.'

Another massive bolt of lightning lit the sky and huge sparks tumbled down the outside of the bubble.

'No-o,' moaned Wullie again. 'This canny be happening.'

'It is happening,' said Moss, gesticulating at the scene outside. 'Soon the lightning will be controlled by the wizards and they will be aiming it at the place of Perth.'

Even as Moss spoke, the lightning began to move away from the Indestructabubble towards houses near the burning football stadium. Great explosions of earth marked its progress. The air was bending and shimmering as if being pushed by an invisible force.

'What *is* that?' Maddie's voice was almost drowned by a thunderous explosion.

'Waves of stopping power,' shouted Moss. 'From the bubble. Can stop anything: combustion carriages, flying machines, projectile firing weapons. Nothing can penetrate.'

'What's it made of?' asked Roger, roaring to be heard.

'The main thing—'

'Never mind what it's made of!' Maddie screamed, hands covering her ears. 'What are they going to do next?'

The dwarf turned and looked at Maddie. 'When lightning has destroyed everything in its path, the Indestructabubble is removed. Dwarves and ogres will attack under Leatherhead's orders. The only thing that can halt the commencement of slaughter is the hammer in Roger's possession.'

Roger rubbed his face with both hands. 'How . . . how do we get to the sword?'

'We need to get closer to Leatherhead Barnstorm,' said Lady Goodroom. 'Drive forward, William. We'll surprise them. Fast as you can!'

'Just haud on a minute,' said Wullie. 'It's been nice to see you all . . .' He opened the van door. 'But I've also got to see the doctor today, my chest, it's awfy bad.' He coughed a couple of times and started to get out of the van.

'You . . .' said Moss, chortling into his beard. 'I love how you companionably banter at time of certain death. Should I survive and you're slaughtered dead to the ground, I'll see that the Wullie wife and weans have an abundance of golden stones.'

Wullie sat back in his seat and closed the door. 'Golden stones, eh?' He put the gear lever into first. 'Abundance? That's an awfy lot, isn't it? Well, ah'm no feeling that bad. I think I'm feeling better. I think I've shrugged it off.' He fastened his seat belt, stepped on the gas and floored it.

As the van shot forward, Roger took the hammer out of his pocket and held it tightly.

The van gathered speed.

'Make horn noise, Wullie,' said Moss, slapping his hands on the front panel. 'All make noise. Switch on the speaking-box, and use your shouting voices.'

The van began to race along the carriageway. The windows were wound down. Everyone began screaming and shouting as loudly as they could. Wullie pressed the horn and switched on the radio.

The van reached the first square of dwarves and swept past the startled faces. Ahead, Leatherhead Barnstorm and Tobias Undercut turned to face the noise. Queen Gwri was standing at the head of her army.

'Aim there!' bellowed Moss, jumping up and down on the floor of the van. 'Strike there!' He leaned forward and struck the fascia panel with both fists.

'No bother, wee man!' yelled Wullie, hunched over the steering wheel. 'But watch the damage. That's my living you're punching.'

Leatherhead Barnstorm raised the Doomstone Sword and pointed it at the van. A beam of brilliant white light shot out of the sword.

'I canny see!' Wullie yelled, shielding his eyes with one hand and slamming on the brakes.

The van skidded right. It flew sideways and hit the safety barrier. Air bags exploded and Roger was thrown against Lady Goodroom, his nose squishing into her armpit. Moss flew forward and smashed head first through the windscreen.

'That's bad,' said Wullie, from behind a deflating air bag. 'The wee fella wisnae wearing a seat belt.'

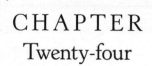

CHAPTER
Twenty-four

'Where did he go?' Roger asked, staring through the space where the windscreen had been. 'Do you think he's . . . ?' His voice trembled.

'I'm no sure,' said Wullie, releasing his seat belt and struggling out from behind the air bag. 'I'll have a look.' He opened his door and jumped out of the van. Lady Goodroom, Maddie and Roger climbed out the other side. They were immediately surrounded by spear-wielding gorefiends.

Roger could see Queen Gwri standing beside her army. Her face was completely blank, her eyes staring off into the distance. Leatherhead and Tobias, talking furiously to each other, were striding towards the prisoners.

Queen Gwri's head twitched. She caught Roger's eye and gave him just the beginning of a smile, then quickly looked away again.

Roger hooked the hammer into his trouser belt and pulled his jumper over it. It was ready, just in case.

'Wait, gorefiends!' yelled Leatherhead Barnstorm, the Doomstone Sword on his shoulder. 'Do not kill them yet.' He looked back at Queen Gwri. 'They should *already* be dead! There is treachery here. I will have the truth of this before they die.'

'The Queen betrayed you,' said Tobias Undercut, as they reached the prisoners. 'That is the only explanation.' He hunched his massive shoulders and glowered menacingly.

Lady Goodroom stepped towards her former butler and stared into his eyes. She turned her head and body slightly to the right, and then swung a punch at the butler's face. Tobias staggered back, holding his nose. He tripped over his feet and crashed to the ground.

'Betrayed?' screamed Lady Goodroom, launching herself at the figure on the ground. '*You* shot my husband!'

There was a noise like an over-inflated beach ball bursting as Tobias took the full weight of Lady Goodroom landing on him. They lay together for a few moments, wobbling precariously, then Tobias grabbed Lady Goodroom and flung her to one side. He stood up, face scarlet and nose bleeding. Roaring, he swung his arms across his body and stamped his feet.

Maddie ran to her aunt. 'Are you all right?'

Wullie stepped forward and placed himself between the raging butler and Lady Goodroom.

'Eh, just haud on,' said Wullie, sticking out his chin. 'Where I come from, you're no allowed tae hurt lassies.'

'Get out of my way,' snarled Tobias Undercut, and he swung his right arm in a vicious sweeping blow at Wullie's head.

Wullie ducked under the punch, caught the butler's wrist and pushed his other hand hard against the elbow now facing him. Tobias spun round, hit the crash barrier and catapulted over it.

'Well done, William!' said Lady Goodroom, as Maddie helped her to stand. 'Where did you learn to do that?'

'Oh, I was in the army, mam,' said Wullie. 'Learned a lot about—'

There was a roar as Tobias climbed back over the barrier. 'You're a dead man!' he screamed, swinging his arms in the air like a demented gorilla.

'Oh, fancy yerself, do you?' Wullie raised his fists and started to shuffle his feet.

'Careful, William,' said Lady Goodroom. 'He used to be a—'

Wullie danced forward and unleashed a flurry of blows. None of the punches seemed to have the slightest effect on Tobias.

'Had enough, eh?' Wullie danced from side to side, pummelling the big man's head and body.

Tobias grunted and swung his right fist in a wide circle, smashing through Wullie's raised arms, hitting him on the chest. Wullie flew backwards, scattering a line of dwarves as he crashed to the ground.

Two dwarves grabbed Wullie under the arms and lifted him to his feet. 'Hit him with a rock,' muttered one of the dwarves. 'It's the only chance you have.'

'Use a big rock,' said the other dwarf, wiping at dirt on Wullie's trousers.

'Ah don't need nothing, just watch this,' said Wullie, fists up, bobbing and weaving again.

Leatherhead Barnstorm walked forward and swung the Doomstone Sword. The flat of the blade struck Wullie across the head and he collapsed without making a sound.

'Enough!' bellowed Leatherhead, turning from the unconscious man to Lady Goodroom, Maddie and Roger. 'You'll all have the sleep of death now.' He waved the sword. 'Ogres, to me! Wizards, remove the Indestructabubble!'

Ogres began moving on to the carriageway. The dwarves, with Queen Gwri, remained standing where they were, staring straight ahead. Dwarf wizards scurried about chanting and waving wands. The Indestructabubble blinked off.

'Take that away,' Leatherhead roared, pointing the sword at the crashed van.

The largest ogre threw back his head and made a loud *keening* noise. A dragon swooped down and clasped the van's roof in its talons. There was a metallic screeching as the dragon tightened its grip and the van lifted off the ground. The dragon climbed into the sky. It broke through the clouds and vanished.

Roger couldn't help wondering where a dragon would dump a wrecked van.

'Now, this one dies,' said Leatherhead, standing over Wullie. He raised the sword in both hands and was just about to swing the killing blow when—

'King Golmar's Braces!' roared a voice.

And Moss appeared, launching himself from the top of the crash barrier. His little legs pedalled furiously as he flew through the air. He thumped on to Leatherhead's back and knocked him stumbling and jerking forward like a mad marionette. The Doomstone Sword flew out of Leatherhead's hands, spinning backwards. It fell point down outside the safety barrier.

Moss landed on his feet, pulled out his axes and crouched.

Leatherhead staggered to a stop. He turned round

and unsheathed his battle-axe. The two dwarves faced each other.

'Finally,' said Moss, 'we end this. Dwarf weapons. Dwarf against dwarf.'

'The Frog Gobbing Cup should've been mine,' snarled Leatherhead.

'Never!' Moss roared back. 'You gob like a mumblecrusted saddle-goose. Natterjack!'

Both dwarves limped closer. There was a brief pause, and then Moss attacked.

There was a great *oohing* and *aahing* from the dwarf army; some sat down, some leaned against their weapons, some got out baccy pipes and lit them. The gorefiends lowered their spears and turned to watch the battle.

The ferocity of the fight was incredible. Moss's arms were like pistons as his small axes rained blow after blow against Leatherhead's battle-axe. Clashing metal rang out and sparks flew as the onslaught continued unabated. Leatherhead blocked and parried, frantically trying to find a way to counter the furious attack as he was driven backwards.

Two gorefiends rushed Moss from either side. Without so much as a glance at them, Moss sliced one in half and killed the other with a sweeping back swipe. There was applause from the dwarf army and the giants banged their tree-clubs on the ground. Even some of the watching gorefiends nodded in approval.

'Look,' said Maddie, pointing.

Tobias Undercut was creeping away from the fight, heading towards the sword on the other side of the barrier.

Maddie started to move. Roger grabbed her arm. 'I'll go.' He began to run, one hand holding on to the hammer at his waist. He felt a sudden flood of hope. *If he could just get to the sword first!*

The nearest gorefiend's ears waggled. It turned round and raised its spear.

'Ah,' said Maddie, stepping right up to the point of the spear. 'Good, I was looking for you. I wanted to ask you a question. Are you heavy?'

The gorefiend put its head to one side and twitched. 'I'm afraid that I do not understand your question.'

'Well,' said Maddie. 'Say I put my hands here and here.' She put both hands wide apart on the wooden shaft of the gorefiend's spear and gripped it tightly in her fists. 'Could I lift you like this? Or are you too heavy?'

'I am—'

Maddie hauled on the spear and swung the gorefiend over her shoulder. It went flying off.

'*Oh, youuuu— Aaaaaagrgh!*' shrieked the gorefiend, as it disappeared.

Tobias saw what was happening and began lumbering faster.

Roger and the butler reached the safety barrier together. Roger jumped up, one foot on the barrier, then pushed himself over and sprinted forward while Tobias was still struggling to get over.

Roger pulled the Doomstone Sword out of the ground and swung round – just as something struck him on the head. There was an explosive red flash.

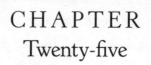

CHAPTER
Twenty-five

Roger gently touched his head. There was a large lump just above his eyebrow. He was lying on the ground, with Tobias Undercut standing over him.

Two gorefiends, carrying the Doomstone Sword between them, scurried back towards the fight on the other side of the barrier.

'What hit me?' asked Roger, wincing at the pain.

'This,' said Tobias Undercut, shoving the fake hammer with the gold band into Roger's face. 'Good shot, eh?' He bent down and grabbed the scruff of Roger's neck and hauled him to his feet. 'Now move,' he said, stuffing the haft of the hammer into his waistband.

Roger stumbled forward. He could see Leatherhead Barnstorm desperately trying to hold off a whirlwind of ringing axe blows from Moss.

The gorefiends carrying the sword reached the fighting dwarves.

'*Master!*'

'*Sword!*'

Leatherhead screamed and took one hand off his battle-axe. He stretched his arm backwards, his podgy fingers wriggling frantically. 'To me!' he yelled to his servants, as Moss renewed his attack.

Moss battered Leatherhead's battle-axe to one side and stepped up to deliver a killer blow . . . just as the gorefiends placed the hilt of the Doomstone Sword into Leatherhead's hand.

'You have it, master!' screeched one of the gorefiends.

Moss, immediately immobilised, stopped fighting. He dropped his axes and stood, chest heaving, then slowly backed away with his head lowered.

Leatherhead staggered, gasping. He tried to raise the sword but could barely hold the point off the ground.

Behind Moss, Roger could see the others, surrounded by gorefiends.

'I said *move*,' said Tobias, pushing Roger in the back. He shoved him all the way up to the barrier.

Leatherhead twisted round to look at him. 'I'm – in – charge now,' he wheezed, as Roger was made to climb over the barrier back on to the road.

Moss caught Roger's eye, and gave the slightest of nods. He mouthed one word: '*Destroyer.*'

Roger nodded back. His head was sore and he

thought his eye was swelling up but he felt strangely calm as he trudged over to join his companions. There was a crazy, dangerous idea forming in his mind. Lady Goodroom was holding her arm and Maddie was rubbing her leg; there were several burn marks on the road.

'Are you all right, Roger?' asked Lady Goodroom, looking up. 'That swine could have killed you.'

'Shut up!' bellowed Tobias. 'You two. Kneel!'

Roger dropped to his knees beside Maddie.

'That wee rat-face there,' said Maddie, pointing at a grinning gorefiend, 'kicked my leg. Look, it's all scratched.'

'*I said*, shut up.' Tobias looked at Moss. 'On your knees.'

'No,' answered Moss. 'Not for you.'

'Then I'll make you,' said Tobias, moving closer.

'Silence!' gasped Leatherhead Barnstorm. 'I am going to kill him. No final prayers or goodbyes. *He dies now!*'

'Do it, then,' shouted Moss. 'You cowardly spit-frog.'

'With great pleasure,' said Leatherhead, just managing to point the Doomstone Sword at Moss. 'At last . . . *I* end you.'

'I had the beating of you,' said Moss, pulling his shoulders back defiantly. 'You were only saved by the sword.'

'I was playing with you,' whined Leatherhead,

swinging the sword back. 'Letting you think you were winning.'

'Oh, *shut up!*' said Roger. He was kneeling, but his voice rang out clearly. 'You're an ugly little twerp with a big sword and a bigger mouth.'

The sword paused mid-swing.

'Well spoken, Roger,' chuckled Moss. 'Your name-calling is admirable. He *is* an ugly little twerp.'

'The worst in the world,' said Maddie, grinning. 'Twerpiest and ugliest I've ever seen.'

Wullie came to at that moment, and raised his head off the ground. 'Ugly wee b—'

'Shut mouths!' screamed Leatherhead, swinging the Doomstone Sword away from Moss and pointing it at Roger. 'You dare speak again!'

Roger raised his head, blinked his sore eye several times and looked at Leatherhead.

'You're the droppings from a cow's bottom. You've got a face like a big pancake of poo. You're like a warty toad who's been hit on the face by a frying pan filled with ugly warts.'

Leatherhead swung the sword over his shoulder and brought it whistling down towards Roger's head.

Using his hands and feet, Roger pushed himself back as hard as he could. The tip of the blade sliced past his face and cut deep into the tarmac. Now the Doomstone Sword's blade was buried to its hilt in the road.

Leatherhead gave it a tug, and it began to slide it out. At that moment, Roger stood up and pulled the hammer from his belt.

Leatherhead grunted in surprise and pulled harder.

With the blade almost free, Roger stepped forward and struck the Doomstone Sword with the hammer.

There was a flash of blue light and a crackling, like ice breaking. The blade of the sword shattered.

A great sigh went up from the assembled dwarves, followed by a general muttering, shuffling and clanking of weapons. Queen Gwri spoke quickly to the nearest dwarf soldier, who nodded and ran towards the ogres. She then walked forward and held up a restraining hand as Moss, grinning wickedly, moved towards Leatherhead.

'Please wait,' said the Queen. She smiled. 'My beloved.'

Leatherhead Barnstorm stared at the hilt of the broken sword clasped in his hands. 'How did—?' He looked at Tobias, who fumbled at his waist and pulled out the hammer with the gold band and held it up. 'We have possession . . . you can't . . .'

'But look what I've got,' said Roger, holding up the real hammer.

Leatherhead looked from one hammer to another,

back and forward for several moments. He shook his head and turned to the dwarves and ogres. 'Wizards, replace the Indestructabubble!' He held up the remains of the sword. 'Death to the race of humans. Forward!'

There was no movement from the dwarf army.

'I speak,' screamed Leatherhead, waving the sword hilt above his head. 'See, I have the Doomstone Sword. Obey me.'

'It has been rendered as useless as murfles on a porker's backside,' said Mossbelly MacFearsome. 'No one will follow your path.'

Leatherhead spluttered for a moment and then threw what was left of the sword at Moss.

Moss ducked.

'Desist!' shouted Queen Gwri. 'Moss, come to my side.'

Moss hunched forward and began pawing the ground with his right foot. His fists were tightly clenched and he was growling.

'Moss,' said Queen Gwri in a quieter voice. 'Come to my side. The treachery is rectified. Everything is now in place.' She spoke louder. 'My orders must be obeyed – *for your own safety*. Now, please!'

Moss straightened slowly, then walked over to stand beside his Queen.

Roger glanced at the dwarf army; there was something strange about them. They were standing or sitting in a very relaxed manner, some were talking quietly and some appeared to be singing or whistling without making any noise. They kept glancing up at the sky. Roger looked up too, but could see nothing unusual – just the dark clouds breaking and rays of sunshine beginning to shine through.

Nonetheless, he slowly began backing away from Leatherhead until he reached Moss.

'You –' Queen Gwri pointed at Leatherhead – 'have betrayed dwarves and ogres, dragons *and* humans. You have made creatures from dead humans. And you –' she pointed at the butler – 'have betrayed, stolen and tried to murder.'

'Lies! Lies! False truth!' Spittle flew from Leatherhead's mouth as he jumped up and down, shaking with rage. The gorefiends were gathering around Leatherhead and Tobias in a protective circle. 'I will not be robbed again! The Frog Gobbing—'

Roger thought he heard a faint whistling noise. He looked up. This time, he *could* see something . . . The whistling was growing louder. Roger stared at the thing hurtling out of the sky. It looked like—

'*Look out!*' shrieked Roger.

At the very last moment, almost at the second of impact, both Tobias and Leatherhead looked up.

But it was too late.

Wullie's white van smashed down on Leatherhead Barnstorm, Tobias Undercut and the gorefiends. Then the van exploded.

The impact of the explosion made Roger take several steps backwards. He raised his arms to ward off the heat blast.

A solitary gorefiend walked out of the flames.

'Ouch!' it said as it pitched forward on to the carriageway. 'I didn't see that coming.'

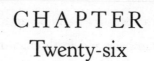

CHAPTER
Twenty-six

'Wizards,' shouted Queen Gwri. 'Make our departure invisible. Dwarves, return to your homes. Ogres, to your sleep.'

'How long do we have to sleep now?' rumbled the largest ogre.

'One hundred and thirty-seven human years left,' said Queen Gwri.

'Hardly seems worth the bother,' grumbled the ogre. *'We'll be up again in no time.'*

'Go,' said Gwri. 'It is short for you but long in the life of humans. Go. I will see you soon.'

The ogres began to walk away. They stamped on the crash barrier, trampling it flat, and threw their tree-clubs into the fields. Dragons followed the ogres, circling in the sky above them.

'Queen,' shouted a dwarf wizard. 'Humans coming!' He pointed towards the burning football stadium where fire engines were arriving.

'Dwarves!' Gwri raised her voice. 'Back to your underground homes.'

The dwarf army turned and began to march up the hill. Wizards ran back and forth chanting and waving wands.

'They'll never get away in time,' said Roger. 'There's too many!'

But just as Roger spoke, the dwarf army began to disappear. Dwarf columns were walking into a shimmering hillside and vanishing. Within minutes, all the dwarves had completely melted away except for Queen Gwri, Moss and two dwarf soldiers holding the pieces of the broken Doomstone Sword.

Queen Gwri stood in front of Lady Goodroom, Maddie and Wullie.

'My good friend,' said Queen Gwri to Lady Goodroom. 'You are an excellent Witchwatcher. Your loyal service is appreciated and shall be rewarded.' She dropped her voice. 'We must redouble our efforts to bring about a reconciliation before time runs out.'

Lady Goodroom smiled. 'Of course. And glad to have been of service, your majesty.' She leaned forward and spoke quietly. 'Would you really have made him King, by Royal dwarf law?'

'Oh no,' replied the Queen. 'It is not in our law. Not

possible. But he didn't know that.' She gave a small smile and spoke softly. 'Not very bright, you know.'

Lady Goodroom laughed. 'Same time next month, tea and tipsycake?'

Queen Gwri smiled and nodded. She turned to Maddie. 'You will make a great Witchwatcher in the future time. You would also be a worthy dwarf, for you have many of the attributes: impetuosity, no regard for safety and a thirst for violence.'

Maddie relaxed her grip on Wullie. 'I enjoyed it, thank you,' she said, giving a bad imitation of a curtsy. 'Quite a lot.'

Wullie slumped sideways and slipped out of Lady Goodroom's grasp. He crashed to the ground and groaned loudly.

As Lady Goodroom and Maddie tried to lift Wullie, the dwarf queen turned to Roger. 'You are a noble human, Roger. You gave much to help Captain Moss. You're brave, resourceful and cunning. You are a true warrior, and worthy of the title, Destroyer. Go home now. Return to your maternal one.'

Roger smiled and gave a slight nod, but did not speak; he had a lump in his throat.

'And you,' said Queen Gwri to Wullie, who was just about up on his feet again. 'Another noble human. I hear that you have a Wullie-wife and weans to supply with food and items of little consequence. Go to them.' She scooped up a handful of pebbles and held them out – gleaming gold – to Wullie.

Lady Goodroom heaved Wullie upright.

'No bother, your queenship,' said Wullie, almost falling again, but still able somehow to take the gold from the dwarf queen and stuff it into a pocket.

'Your ladyship.' Moss thumped his right fist against his chest and bowed towards Lady Goodroom and Maddie, who were struggling hard to keep Wullie on his feet. 'My pleasure to fight at your side, Witchwatcher, and you, young human female, Mad-one.'

'Maddie,' said Maddie, laughing. 'My name is Maddie, but I'll take Mad-one. That's good, a joke coming from you. Next thing you'll be buying yourself a tractor.'

Moss growled and looked at Roger. He held out his hand.

Roger, shyly, went to shake it.

Moss slapped Roger's hand away. 'Hammer!' he snapped.

'Oh! Here it is . . .' Roger pulled out the hammer and handed it to the dwarf. 'One thing. When you came over the crash barrier . . . I thought you couldn't attack the bearer of the Doomstone Sword?'

'I wasn't attacking him,' said Moss. 'I was jumping in the air. Landed on him by accident.'

'Glad you did,' said Roger.

'Some day, though, if we are lucky,' said Moss, 'we may still have the chance to fall in battle together, perish as true warriors should, brothers in arms.'

Roger laughed. 'That's nice. I'll look forward to that.' He bent down a little and looked into the dwarf's eyes. 'And I *was* going to dig you out – eventually.'

Moss smiled, an enormous smile that lit up his torn, bleeding face. 'Goodbye, plum,' he said, holding out his hand again. 'Let's make a handband.'

'Oh,' said Roger. 'Goodbye, prune.' He shook the outstretched hand and smiled back.

'You *are* a good companion.' Moss looked serious. 'But your insults could be improved. Being likened to a toad and a profusion of warts are great compliments to a dwarf.' He let go of Roger's hand and gave a very large and deliberate wink.

Roger, still smiling, winked back and then yelped with pain as it was his swollen eye he had used.

Queen Gwri, Mossbelly MacFearsome and the two remaining dwarves turned and walked away. They passed through the shimmering hill and vanished. Roger, Maddie and Lady Goodroom stood for a moment looking at nothing, they could hear sirens wailing in the distance.

'I never got to ask him,' said Roger, still gazing after the departed dwarves.

'Ask him what?' Lady Goodroom staggered a little, as Wullie slumped in her arms again.

'What happens to the frogs?' asked Roger. 'The ones they use for the Frog Gobbing.'

'Oh, they're fine,' said Lady Goodroom. 'They puff themselves up and bounce along the ground. They enjoy it.'

'And how about the sore nail on the twisted princess?' asked Maddie. 'What's *that* all about?'

'Later, dear,' said Lady Goodroom, as she and Maddie lowered Wullie to the ground. 'I'll tell you all about it later.'

Wullie moaned.

'William,' said Lady Goodroom, kneeling down beside him. She patted his face. 'William, William, are you still with us?'

Wullie moaned again, and his eyelids fluttered.

'William, can you hear me?' asked Lady Goodroom. 'I'm going to help you with a little spell.'

Wullie's eyes blinked several times before opening.

'Aye,' he mumbled. 'I can hear you.' He sat up and looked around. 'What hit me?'

'The Doomstone Sword,' said Lady Goodroom. 'Lucky it was the flat bit.'

'That's me,' said Wullie, gently touching the back of his head. 'I'm aye lucky.'

An ambulance came screeching up the carriageway and stopped at a tree blocking the road. More fire engines were racing towards the football stadium.

'Would you look at that?' said Wullie, pointing at his wrecked and burning van. 'How am ah gonny feed my family now? The wife'll kill me.'

Maddie began to giggle. Roger and Lady Goodroom began to giggle too. They held on to each other and laughed and laughed. Wullie started to join in.

'Oh, my heid's sore,' chortled Wullie. 'What are we laughing at?'

'So's mine,' said Roger, almost sobbing. 'I don't know!'

By the time the paramedics reached them, they were all laughing hysterically.

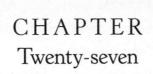

CHAPTER
Twenty-seven

'Mrs Botting and Mrs McKeek don't remember anything,' said Roger. 'But every time they see me, they cross the road.' He laughed. 'It's quite funny. One minute they're talking away as usual, then they see me and they're off as fast as they can go.'

Roger was sitting in the back of a new Jaguar saloon as it purred through Edinburgh. He was between Lady Goodroom and Maddie and they were all looking at the castle dominating the grey skyline. It was four weeks since the fight outside Perth. Or, as the dwarves were calling it: The Battle of Wullie's Van.

'There's a lot who don't remember,' said Lady Goodroom, ducking to watch the castle passing the nearside window. 'I couldn't contribute much, my magic is too limited. It's a combination of things: wizards' spells, the magic the dwarves have been spreading since, and of course the story the government put out about escaping gas causing hallucinations during earthquakes. And perhaps people just don't want to remember, scared that others may laugh at them.' She leaned forward and tapped the driver's shoulder. 'Driver! Driver! Slow down, please. Thank you.'

The car crawled round a corner as Roger, Maddie and Lady Goodroom gazed out of the window.

'Mmmm,' said Lady Goodroom. 'Go round again, driver, please.'

They all settled back as the car gathered speed.

'And the boy?' asked Lady Goodroom. 'The bully you had the fight with? The one Moss almost killed?'

'Hugh,' said Roger. 'Nothing. He runs a mile whenever he sees me. All the kids think I'm great for stopping his bullying.' He nodded. 'And my mum doesn't say anything about it. She seems to have forgotten what happened. Strange. But she's happy now that Dad's home for good, thanks to his new job working for the Forestry Commission.' He smiled at Lady Goodroom. 'Thank you.'

'Amazing what a little influence can do,' said Lady Goodroom, laughing. 'And I'm getting a new library built too. Now, I think we should do it, don't you?'

'Yes,' said Roger, nodding.

'Let's,' said Maddie. She gently punched Roger on the arm.

'Right,' said Lady Goodroom. 'We'll need to walk.

When it's over, I'll go and collect Penrose from his check-up at the hospital and then drop you off at home, Roger.'

'I'm glad he's a lot better,' said Roger.

'When I think how close I came to losing him . . .' said Lady Goodroom. Her voice trailed off and she dabbed her eyes.

'It's all right,' said Maddie, leaning over Roger and squeezing Lady Goodroom's arm. 'He's fine now, we're all fine. Well, except for the two *unidentified* people killed in the earthquakes – our butler and Leatherhead Barnstorm. Oh, and the man in the burning car who jumped into the bushes and got a broken leg when the other two men jumped on top of him. And all the people who missed the football match when the stadium burned down.'

Lady Goodroom sniffed, and then gave a little laugh. 'And your two ladies, Roger – Mrs Botting and Mrs McKeek.'

Roger laughed. 'If you had seen their faces when Moss stood up waving his axe and screaming at them – the funniest thing I've ever seen. But not at the time.'

'I'd like to have seen that.' Lady Goodroom laughed again.

The car reached the old part of the city. Seagulls were shrieking overhead.

'Stop here, driver,' said Lady Goodroom, looking up

215

at the circling gulls. 'They are not as big as dragons, but they're a lot noisier.' She pointed up the road. 'There's hardly anyone about at this time in the morning. If we're lucky no one will see us. It'll get a lot of publicity. People will try to pull it out, but nothing will shift it now. Just enough magic left in it. Maybe they'll wonder why it's there. Try to find the ancient records and realise how much time they've wasted. How little time *we* have left to sort things out.'

Roger nodded. 'Hope so. If not, we'll have to help them remember.' He bent down, picked up the tartan blanket and carefully pulled it open. 'They made a super job re-forging it,' he said, looking at the repaired sword for the umpteenth time. 'You can't see any marks at all.' He folded the cloth back over the Doomstone Sword and looked at Lady Goodroom and Maddie. 'Ready?'

'Yes,' said Lady Goodroom. 'But before we do it, are you still sure you want to join Maddie? To be a Warlockwatcher?' She looked into Roger's eyes. 'It's a lot of work. Spells to learn, reports to send, big responsibilities.'

'I'll help you to catch up,' said Maddie. 'And I can show you how to fight properly.'

'Very sure,' said Roger, returning Lady Goodroom's gaze. 'About the Warlockwatcher bit anyway. Not so sure about being taught by your crazy niece, though.'

'Good,' said Lady Goodroom, as she held out her hands to prevent Maddie punching Roger. 'Driver, this is it. Wait here and keep the engine running, just in case.'

Wullie hopped out and opened the passenger door next to the pavement. 'Righto, your mamship,' he said, holding the door and bowing low. 'Motor running for fast getaway, nae bother. But what's this, *driver*? Yer a right cheeky witch, so you are. I'm a part-time butler and part-time bodyguard, with a wee bit of driving thrown in. I like what you called me when you offered me the job, *your factotum*. I might even change my name to that.'

Lady Goodroom, Maddie and Roger got out of the car, chuckling. They stood on the pavement looking up the cobbled road. Roger hugged the blanket holding the sword.

'Come along, children,' said Lady Goodroom, striding forward. 'Please wait here,' she shouted back at Wullie, standing beside the car. 'If anyone questions you, tell them that you are my PFP.'

'What's that stand for?' yelled Wullie.

'Personal Factotum Protector,' Lady Goodroom shouted back. 'You're in charge of all my security.'

'That's better, your ladywitch,' said Wullie, standing to attention and saluting. 'I like the sound of that.'

'I think . . . here,' said Lady Goodroom, puffing a little. 'We're near enough to the entrance. People will see it here. Yes, this'll do nicely.'

Roger and Maddie stopped at the spot indicated.

Lady Goodroom nodded. Roger knelt down and unfolded the blanket again. He stood up and held the Doomstone Sword with the tip resting on the cobblestones. Maddie placed her hands on top of Roger's, and then pinched the back of his hand.

'The trouble this thing's caused over the centuries,' said Lady Goodroom. 'Nothing but bother since it was created.'

'It will be safe here,' said Maddie, swaying a little as Roger pushed against her. She giggled. 'If they can't get their hands on it, it can't cause any more trouble.'

'Go ahead, children,' said Lady Goodroom, smiling.

Roger and Maddie pushed down – and the Doomstone Sword slid into the stone, almost to the hilt.

They let go and stepped back.

Lady Goodroom mumbled a few words and waved her hands over the sword.

There was a deep, underground rumble. The ground shook.

'What's that?' Roger staggered from one foot to the other.

'A tremor,' said Lady Goodroom, arms raised out to the side to steady herself. 'An earthquake.'

The shaking stopped. There was a low murmuring sound.

'What—?' Roger shook his head at Lady Goodroom.

'I think we should get out of here,' said Lady Goodroom, stooping to pick up the tartan blanket. 'Come, children, quickly!' She started to stride back down the cobbled road.

'Do you think the Doomstone Sword made that happen?' asked Roger, catching up with Lady Goodroom. 'I thought the dwarves told you its power was gone. That the magic leaked out when I broke it?'

'They did,' answered Lady Goodroom, walking faster.

'What's down there?' asked Maddie.

'Nothing that I know of,' said Lady Goodroom. 'Just an extinct volcano.'

'Do you—?' Maddie ran in front of Lady Goodroom and stopped. 'Do you think that we disturbed something?'

'I really don't know.' Lady Goodroom turned Maddie round and pushed her forward. 'We'll find out. Now I *really do* think we should get away from here. William's waiting for us.'

The ground shook again as they approached the car, another deep rumble.

They began to run.

Wullie was standing with the car doors open. Beside him was Mossbelly MacFearsome. The dwarf disappeared – then seconds later reappeared.

'Hurry up!' yelled Wullie, as Moss blinked on and off. 'Wee hairybottom's gotta message for you.'

Moss appeared again, unfastening the see-through covert cloak from his neck. He stuffed it into the satchel on his hip and climbed into the car.

There was an even louder rumble.

Maddie was first to the car, throwing herself on to the back seat beside Moss. Roger followed a second later. Lady Goodroom heaved herself in and collapsed on the cushion. Wullie slammed the door shut, jumped into the driver's seat and had the car moving before his own door was closed.

'What are you doing here, Captain MacFearsome?' asked Lady Goodroom, panting, as Roger and Maddie fussed around Moss.

'Trying to stop what you were doing!' said Moss, flapping away Roger and Maddie. 'But I was too late.'

'Stop what?' said Lady Goodroom. 'You knew what we were doing, we told you. We were just placing the Doomstone Sword in the ground before Edinburgh wakes up.'

'That's what I tried to stop,' said Moss gravely. 'It's *where* you've placed it. You've unleashed a nocturnal nightmare. The world is in danger!'

'What are you talking about?' asked Roger. 'Nothing could be worse than Leatherhead and his gorefiends.'

'Much worse,' said Moss, shaking his head. 'I fear you have awakened Redcap the Goblin Chief from his prison beneath the castle. This is very bad.'

'What's so bad about a goblin?' asked Maddie. 'What could a goblin do that's so bad?'

'Do?' shouted Moss. 'I'll tell you what he can do . . .'

There was silence for a moment.

'*What?*' Three voices shouted as one.

'Humph.' Moss glared back at the three staring faces. 'Well, he can control humans, and . . .'

'*And what?*'

'He can open a portal to another dimension and launch a goblin invasion to conquer the Earth!'

'Oh no,' said Lady Goodroom, slumping back in her seat.

'Wow,' said Maddie, her eyes flashing as she punched Roger on the arm. 'Well, we'd better stop him, then.'

'Oh, badgers' bums, not again,' sighed Roger.

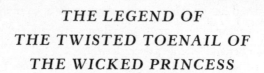

THE LEGEND OF
THE TWISTED TOENAIL OF
THE WICKED PRINCESS

(as related by Lady Goodroom)

Long, long ago there lived a beautiful dwarf princess. Unfortunately, she had a spiteful, brutish nature: she was cruel to animals, nasty to the elderly, and enjoyed pinching baby dwarves on their bottoms until they howled.

One night, an owl flew into her bedchamber, and bit the big toe on one of her backwards-facing feet. As the princess awoke, screaming, the owl spoke to her and said that she was being punished for her wicked, twisted ways. From that moment on she was cursed – the nail on her bitten toe moved. It twisted and turned and pressed and squeezed, and felt as if a hundred tiny needles were being pushed into her flesh.

The wisest dwarves in the land studied the twisted toenail. Many cures were tried. Nothing worked. The princess was in constant pain.

One bleak midwinter, not having slept for days, the princess sent for the finest swordsdwarf in the entire kingdom and begged him to cut off her toe. She promised him riches beyond his wildest dreams and swore an oath never to be cruel again. With one precise blow the toe was sliced from her foot. There was no blood, and the skin immediately healed over the wound.

The princess, free of pain at last, picked up her severed toe, kissed it, and then hurled it into a blazing fire. Giggling madly, she ordered her guards to throw the swordsdwarf out of the castle, without any reward. She then went straight to her bedchamber and fell into a deep sleep.

The following morning, when the chambermaid went to waken her, the princess was not in her room. The castle was searched from top to bottom but she was nowhere to be found. The only clue was that, outside the bedchamber where the princess slept, there were deep animal scratches on the castle walls. The princess was never seen again. And, when the fireplace in the castle was cleaned, the severed toe was found in the ashes – completely unharmed.

Over the centuries that followed, the toe became a venerated relic. Before any sacred oath was sworn, it became the custom to kiss the toe. Anyone breaking his or her oath would meet with a terrible fate. On stormy nights, when the wind was howling through the rafters and rattling windows, dwarf mothers would tell their children that the moaning of the wind was the Wicked Princess looking for her lost toe.

Nowadays, most dwarves believe that this is just an old faery story. Dwarf-lore. No one can even remember what the princess's real name was or when all this was meant to have happened. What is *not* disputed, however, is that something that looks exactly like a big toe is still displayed in the Great Hall of Dwarven Ancestry, and that no dwarf would ever kiss the Twisted Toenail of the Wicked Princess and swear an oath unless they really, *really* meant it . . .

ACKNOWLEDGEMENTS

Chloe Sackur, Commissioning Editor, Andersen Press
Without this admirable human, our story would not have been told. Her support has been exceptional, and her counsel invaluable.

Sue Cook, Copy Editor
Her ability to fit the correct squiggle-dot symbols onto a writing page, and in the right places, is a wondrous thing to behold.

James Lancett, Cover Artist
His likeness of the great Mossbelly MacFearsome is an excellent facsimile – although, in reality, I am a much better looker.

Kate Grove, Art Director, Andersen Press
She has designed the book with immense skill – a worthy tribute to the great adventure contained within.

Signed today,

𝕸𝖔𝖘𝖘𝖇𝖊𝖑𝖑𝖞 𝕸𝖆𝖈𝕱𝖊𝖆𝖗𝖘𝖔𝖒𝖊

His Royal Whiskers

SAM GAYTON

ILLUSTRATED BY PETER COTTRILL

Something bad has happened to Prince Alexander, the only heir to the mighty Petrossian Empire. Something worse than kidnapping. Something worse than murder. Somehow, the Prince has been miraculously transformed into a fluffy-wuffy kitten.

Why has this terrible catastrophe happened? Who are the boy and girl brewing secret potions down in the palace kitchens? And how are they possibly going to avoid getting their heads chopped off?

'An outstanding story packed with magic and mayhem'
Abi Elphinstone

9781783443826

GABRIEL'S CLOCK

HILTON PASHLEY

Jonathan is the only half-angel, half-demon in the universe, and now the forces of Hell want him for their own purpose.

Aided by a vicar with a broken heart, a big man with a cricket bat and a very rude cat, Jonathan races to find the mysterious Gabriel's Clock. If he doesn't find it then his family and friends will die, but, if he does, then he risks starting a war between Heaven and Hell that could engulf them all.

Gabriel's clock is ticking . . .
and time is running out.

9781783441136

THE GHOST PRISON

JOSEPH DELANEY

Illustrated by Scott M. Fischer

'This is the entrance to the Witch Well and behind that door you'd face your worst nightmare. Don't ever go through there.'

Night falls, the portcullis rises in the moonlight, and young Billy starts his first night as a prison guard. But this is no ordinary prison. There are haunted cells that can't be used, whispers and cries in the night . . . and the dreaded Witch Well. Billy is warned to stay away from the prisoner down in the Witch Well. But who could it be? What prisoner could be so frightening? Billy is about to find out . . .

'Will satisfy the most hardened fan of horror'
The Times

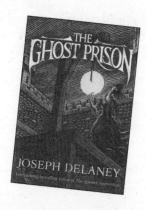

'Spine-tingling'
Love reading

9781783443208